Confessions of a Psychopath

A Novel

Michael Kidwell

Michael Kidwell

Disclaimer

This book contains graphic violence, including cannibalism. Some descriptive narratives may be disturbing or offensive. It is what it is.

Origins

What is reality, truly? Is it an elusive specter that dances on the edges of our perception or a solid, unyielding fortress where the unshakable truths reside? Can we ever fully grasp its intricate fabric, or does it remain a shimmering mirage, shifting with the collective will of those surrounding us?

In the recesses of the human mind, within the labyrinth of visual and audio psychosis, we find a realm where reality becomes a splintered reflection of the world we think we know. For most, these inner landscapes are the territories of hallucinations, personal mirages that evaporate under the scrutiny of objectivity. But for Dr. Allen Creed, a master of the enigmatic psyche, this territory was more than a presumption; it was a kingdom he ventured to conquer.

His forty-year career was a relentless odyssey, a mission to decipher the cryptic language of human consciousness. He was the lifeline for those who would otherwise have met their fate at the hands of justice. Creed saw it as his calling, or perhaps, a predestined path that he tread with unwavering dedication, the torchbearer for those lost in the caverns of their minds.

But there's a toll that such an unwavering pursuit extracts from one's life. The sacrifice was personal, etched in the fading memories of his marriage. Maggie, his faithful partner for twenty-one years, could no longer navigate the treacherous waters of his boundless obsession. With John and Candace in tow, she embarked on a journey that led her away from Creed into a different world, leaving him to traverse the solitary path he had carved for himself.

Maggie had, without hesitation, branded him a deadbeat husband and father. She had no qualms sharing her scathing opinion of him with anyone who would listen, be it their extended family or mutual friends. Dr. Creed, on the other hand, fiercely contested this damning judgment, refusing to wear the deadbeat label.

In his eyes, he had provided everything he could for his family – an idyllic home complete with a swimming pool nestled in a picturesque neighborhood, a trove of the latest computerized gadgets, and more. He could hardly be faulted for being a man many depended on; his expertise sought far and wide. The meager time he spent within the confines of their home was dedicated to poring over the dark tales of criminal case files handed to him by the unforgiving court.

His life was a never-ending procession of these harrowing stories. Dr. Creed was tasked with assessing and testifying on cases involving psychotic defendants who had perpetrated heinous crimes, some of them harboring dark shadows that no ordinary mind could fathom. It was upon his judgment that the fate of these individuals hinged – a lifetime confined to psychiatric institutions or the ever-looming specter of execution. His career was of immense gravity, which he carried with unwavering solemnity.

Within this realm of grim responsibility, Abigail Hammon, the diligent court transcriptionist, was his sole distraction. Both had toiled under the same roof for many years, yet Dr. Creed's interactions with her barely extended beyond work boundaries. He was a professional through and through, a man of business with a no-nonsense approach to his profession.

Unknown to Dr. Creed, Abigail had become an ardent admirer. She had silently pined for him, longing for the moments when they shared the same courtroom. Her heart raced with anticipation whenever he took the stand, a sentiment shared by the entire court. Abigail hung on his every word, enchanted by his expertise and the unruffled manner in which he fielded the prosecution's relentless inquiries, leaving even the most aggressive attorneys disheartened and deflated as they retreated to their seats.

Abigail's infatuation was no secret to her closest friend, Anna, who happened to be Dr. Creed's receptionist. She had been privy to the depths of Abigail's affection, understanding that this yearning would not be quelled by mere proximity. Abigail desired Dr. Creed not as a passing acquaintance but as her partner and lover, her heart's genuine desire beckoning her to a precipice from which there was no return.

Sitting on the cozy front deck of Laura's, the small mom-and-pop bakery that had become their sanctuary, Abigail and Anna basked in the early morning sun. Anna, true to her gossipy nature, was practically bubbling with excitement. She had a secret, and she was terrible at keeping it.

Well aware of Anna's tendency to share news, Abigail initially pretended to be indifferent. She took a slow sip of her espresso, hiding her curiosity behind an air of nonchalance. But as she observed Anna's mounting impatience and fidgeting, she couldn't resist any longer.

With a theatrical sigh, Abigail leaned back, arms crossed, and said, "Alright, Anna, you win. Why are you grinning?"

Anna, leaning in closer with a sly smile, whispered, "I overheard Dr. Creed talking to an attorney yesterday."

Abigail raised an eyebrow, her interest now genuinely piqued. "Just any attorney, or is there more to this?"

Anna, glancing over her shoulder as if checking for eavesdroppers, replied, "Not just any attorney, Abbey. A divorce attorney."

Now, Abbey's curiosity was fully engaged. "That's intriguing. I had no idea Dr. Creed was going through a divorce."

Anna couldn't hold back her delight any longer. "Well, Abbey, his divorce isn't pending; it's done. Dr. Creed is officially a free man."

Abbey grinned but was quick to add, "That's wonderful news, Anna, but I'm not about to swoop in like a vulture the moment his divorce is finalized. We should give him some space."

Anna couldn't resist a mischievous smile. "Just don't give him too much space, my dear. Once the word gets out, you can bet there'll be plenty of single ladies vying for his attention."

As the weeks rolled by, one month turned into two, then three, it became increasingly evident that Dr. Creed was in no hurry to make the first move. The responsibility of initiating non-work-related contact fell squarely on Abbey's shoulders.

Abigail waited for Dr. Creed outside the courtroom, where he busied himself with paperwork and the labyrinthine maze of legal intricacies within. The minutes dragged on, and the wait felt interminable, almost like she was on trial herself. Finally, as the courtroom doors swung open, Abbey's heart raced. There he was, Dr. Allen Creed, walking out into the world beyond those formidable doors and, perhaps, into a new chapter that fate was hinting at.

As Allen strolled past, he flashed a casual grin in Abbey's direction. "Dr. Creed," she called out, her voice tinged with a hint of nervousness.

Allen stopped in his tracks, turning to face her with genuine curiosity. "Yes, Abigail, can I help you?" This marked the first time he'd addressed her by her first name in the two decades she had spent working alongside him.

Stunned by this unprecedented familiarity, Abbey cleared her throat before mustering the courage to ask, "Dr. Creed, would you like to grab a drink after work?"

Allen's smile masked his excitement well. "Where do you have in mind?"

Glancing down at the stack of paperwork she held, Abbey hadn't expected him to agree so readily. After a moment of contemplation, she replied, "How does McCallisters sound to you?"

Although Allen had never set foot in the well-known Irish pub, he enthusiastically replied, "That sounds great. How does six o'clock sound to you?"

Abbey couldn't help but smile, feeling a rush of delight. "That sounds perfect. It's a date."

Regret immediately washed over her for uttering those cliched words, but there was no taking them back.

"Okay, Abigail, it's a date. I'll be there at six," Allen replied, grinning. Despite the awkwardness that briefly lingered, Abbey felt a newfound warmth as she made her way to her office.

Their McCallisters rendezvous was a decade in the past, and their union had blossomed into a loving marriage over the following two years. For both Allen and Abbey, it was as though they had discovered their soulmates.

Returning from an idyllic two-week vacation in the Bahamas, where they reveled in a small beachfront cottage surrounded by swaying palm trees, the real world was a jarring disappointment. Their days had been a delightful tapestry of horseback rides along the shore, sun-soaked afternoons punctuated by Mai Tais, and evenings spent at an open-air restaurant they both adored, with exquisite cuisine, a stellar house band and a diligent staff that had made it an unforgettable escape.

Back in Springfield, Missouri, they knew that the vacation couldn't last forever. The realities of their everyday lives beckoned.

At 9:00 a.m., Allen entered his office, only to find an imposing box adorned with a bow and an envelope taped beside it resting on his desk. Setting his briefcase aside, he sat to examine this intriguing arrival. The box bore a label with the name Zackary Williams; the envelope contained a note.

"Allen, call me before you open the box. I have some explaining to do before you examine the contents. Yours truly, Abraham. PS I hope you enjoyed your vacation."

Allen couldn't help but grin as he realized he hadn't heard from his colleague and old friend, Dr. Abraham Goldberg, in quite some time. Abraham, much like Allen, was a dedicated psychiatrist working with psychiatric patients at Running Springs County Mental Health – a place where they had each channeled their unrelenting energy.

He picked up the phone and dialed Abraham's office. After several rings, Abraham's voice answered, "Hello, this is Dr. Goldberg. How can I be of help?"

Chuckling, Allen responded, "Well, I'm not entirely sure, Abraham. I returned from a fantastic vacation and found your note."

Abraham's laughter echoed through the line. "Good morning, Allen. Did you like the bow? I thought it was a nice touch."

"I thought the bow was just a nice touch, but now it feels like you're sending me Pandora's box, Abe. So, what's the deal with this patient?"

Abraham leaned into the conversation, his tone somber. "It's about one of my patients who will soon become yours. While you were away, I managed to get the paperwork sorted to transfer him to Churchill."

Allen sighed, "It would've been nice to get a heads-up about this patient before he lands in my care."

Abe, understanding Allen's frustration, nodded. "I get it, Allen, I really do, but here's the situation: we're full."

Allen rolled his eyes; the chronic overcrowding issue in mental health facilities was no secret. "All right, I've got nothing on my schedule for tomorrow anyway. I'll come by and do the intake assessment. But you better fill me in now."

Clearing his throat, Abraham began, "His name is Zackary Williams. He's eighteen and was convicted of a gruesome crime. Last year, in July, he murdered his parents, Darleen and Charlie Williams, with an ax. Zackary never denied the murders. He pleaded guilty but never offered any defense. The prosecution initially sought the death penalty, but after I assessed him, I convinced the jury that a long-term psychiatric care facility would be a more humane solution. With time, rehabilitation might be possible."

A hint of admiration crept into Allen's expression. "Well done, my old friend."

Abraham continued, "There's more to it. When law enforcement arrested Williams, he was found standing on the front porch of his house, clutching a young pregnant woman named Sarah Buchanan.

Her husband had reported her missing two weeks prior. She was alive but in horrific shape. Paramedics rushed her to Saint Mary's, where they discovered she had been brutally tortured, presumably by Williams, though she has never spoken or responded to anyone. She remains catatonic."

Concerned, Allen inquired, "What about her baby? Did the child survive?"

Abraham responded, "Yes, the baby survived and lives with her father. On the other hand, Sarah Buchanan resides in a state-funded group home in Missouri."

Allen leaned back in his chair, processing the grim details. "Is there anything else?"

Abraham nodded solemnly. "Much more, I'm afraid. When authorities executed a search warrant on Williams's property, they found something truly horrifying. The cellar of the house contained three freezers. One held the body of Williams's grandfather, and the other two contained the mutilated remains of four women. The bodies had been dismembered, almost like they were packaged for sale. Investigators suspect that the Williams family might have practiced cannibalism."

Allen's expression grew darker as he listened to the disturbing account. "This is beyond anything I've ever encountered. I've dealt with deeply troubled individuals, but this is on another level."

Abraham added, "It gets worse, Allen. Divers found human remains in a pond on the property. Not one set, but twenty-three, and there could be more. The medical examiner determined that all twenty-three victims were female. Here's the kicker—one of the bodies found in the pond was Zackary's biological mother. DNA tests showed no matching DNA between Zackary, Darleen, and Charlie, his supposed parents."

Allen furrowed his brow. "So the couple murdered in the house weren't his parents?"

Abe responded, "Hold on, I'm getting to that part. After digging into Zackary's biological family, investigators found they all live in East Germany. When they contacted his grandparents, it was a rollercoaster of emotions. They confirmed that their daughter, Zackary's mother, along with her twin grandsons and son-in-law, disappeared sixteen years ago while on a three-month camping trip in the US. When they heard Zackary was alive, they were thrilled. But they wanted nothing to do with him as soon as they heard where he was and what he was accused of."

Allen was left stunned by the macabre details of this case. "This is more than a Pandora's box, Abe. It's a nightmare."

Allen's fingers combed through his silver hair as he tried to digest the chilling information Abe had just shared. "Jesus Christ, Abe, a colleague briefly mentioned something about a young man murdering his parents last year, but I didn't think to investigate further. So you're telling me Zackary was the abducted twin?"

Abraham nodded gravely. "That's the prevailing theory. Investigators believe that Zackary may have been kidnapped as a toddler and raised by the Williamses."

"I should have delved into the case, even if only out of morbid curiosity."

Abe offered a perspective. "You wouldn't have found much. Williams confessed to his parents' murders and was convicted. That's all law enforcement shared with the press. Everything else has been under tight wraps. My source told me that investigators are under strict orders to keep further details confidential, sharing only a brief account of Williams's arrest with the media to reassure the Riverview community. Crimes of this magnitude are extremely rare in that area."

Allen nodded. "Small towns tend to think they're immune until something of this scale shakes them to their core. So, do you believe rehabilitation is possible?"

Abraham hesitated. "Allen, I'll be honest. This young man has a complex medley of psychiatric issues. I spent two months with him in daily sessions. I rarely got a word out of him. He doesn't speak. He just sits, eyes locked on the floor. So, no, I'm not optimistic about rehabilitation."

Allen gazed out of his office window, lost in thought. "So, what's your plan, Abe? You're one of the best psychiatrists I know. Why would my professional opinion differ from yours?"

Abraham explained, "Allen, I'm not certain it would, but I didn't want you to be blindsided when this patient lands in your care."

"Fair enough. So, Williams will be here by 9:00 a.m. tomorrow?"

Abe affirmed, "That's the plan. I've arranged for four Corrections deputies and a transport van."

Allen laughed despite the grim situation. "Well, Abe, you sure know how to welcome a man back to work."

"Apologies for the timing, Allen. You'll have to tell me about your vacation one of these days."

"That's a deal, Abe. I'll catch up with you later."

Allen hung up the phone, turning his attention to the box on his desk.

Abe had provided a detailed summary, but Allen wanted to delve into the files and photographs himself. He knew that the crime scene images often offered profound insights into a patient's psyche, serving as a crucial component of his assessment. As a staunch believer in the saying, "A picture speaks a thousand words," he meticulously examined the crime scene photos.

Starting with a satellite image of the Williams residence, Allen noted its isolation deep within the woods, a sinister setting for multiple homicides. Three ponds were marked on the property: one where bodies were discovered (red arrow), another containing miscellaneous debris and vehicles (yellow arrow), and a third where nothing unusual was found (green arrow). Additional red arrows pointed to the house and a small shed to the east, where more evidence of homicide was uncovered.

Allen set the map aside and focused on the crime scene photographs. Images from the front yard displayed a disarray of over a dozen vehicles engulfed by encroaching weeds. Some car hoods were open, exposing their engines, while others had both hoods and doors ajar.

The house itself was a two-story structure in a state of decay. Paint peeled from the walls in long strips, revealing its neglected state. Nature seemed attempting to reclaim the property as wild brambles crept along the house's surface.

Allen continued to scrutinize the photographs. Several depicted Charlie and Darleen Williams, the victims.

Forensic photographs captured Charlie lying in a pool of blood, face up, outside a bedroom. His lifeless face contorted in what seemed like a final act of rage. His chest and abdomen had been gruesomely opened, revealing his internal organs.

It appeared Charlie had a brief moment to defend himself as a handgun lay beside him. A single bullet hole in the floor flagged with a marker, indicated that his shot had missed the intended target by a mere sixteen inches. Blood splatters on the walls and ceiling attested to the brutality of the attack. The scene was a grim tableau of a family's destruction.

The chilling series of photographs continued. Allen's focus shifted to images of Darleen Williams lying at the foot of her blood-soaked bed. Next to her, the murder weapon, a large wood-splitting ax, lay abandoned, presumably left behind by the assailant. Like her husband, Darleen had an expression of rage etched into her lifeless face. Her chest and abdomen displayed identical, gaping wounds, with her intestines spilling onto the floor.

Bloody footprints were visible in the photographs, leading from the room where she lay into the hallway and back out.

A picture captured inside another bedroom revealed a mattress covered in large bloodstains. Four short lengths of rope were attached to the footboard and headboard, each no more than a foot long. Allen concluded that this room was not a typical bedroom but a nightmarish torture chamber.

Further forensic photographs depicted the rest of the house, which was bewilderingly immaculate and adorned with fine antique furnishings, starkly contrasting the decrepit exterior.

Subsequently, the forensic team documented the basement. Two access points led into the dimly lit space. One connected from the living room, while the other, on the house's east side, featured a set of wooden double doors and a flight of ten steps leading to the cellar's depths. Four bare light bulbs hung from the ceiling, each wired to a single electrical line, with frayed strings serving as makeshift switches.

A small, rudimentary cage made from rebar stood in the northwest corner while a chain dangled from its top. Beside the cage sat a stained porcelain bathtub that had clearly seen years of grim use—Allen surmised it had been the site of many, if not all, of the murders on the property.

As Abraham had previously described, three filthy freezers lined the east wall. Two contained sealed plastic bags filled with human flesh, carefully cut and stacked, reminiscent of a grotesque grocery store meat department. The third freezer held the clothed body of an older man with a wide gash across his throat, a fatal wound inflicted by a sharp object.

Beyond the house, near the pond, a makeshift command center was established by forensic investigators. Four blue tarps on the ground held the mud-caked skeletal remains of twenty-three individuals, along with disintegrating clothing articles, painting a grim tableau of a mass atrocity.

Additionally, investigators had extracted five vehicles from the debris pond, along with the dismembered remains of seven more.

The property's horrific revelation painted a picture of an unrelenting killing factory that had operated for many years, sending chills down the spines of those who unearthed the horrifying truth.

As grim as the scene was, Allen couldn't deny the morbid fascination that had taken hold of him. He looked forward to meeting Zackary Williams, hoping he might encourage the young man to reveal the horrifying events that had unfolded on the property. The chilling prospect of unlocking the secrets of this house of horrors intrigued the seasoned psychiatrist.

Allen carefully placed the unsettling crime scene photos back inside the box. For the time being, he had seen enough and wanted to put some mental distance between himself and the gruesome images that now filled his thoughts.

That evening, as rain poured down, Allen pulled into his driveway. He glanced at the box sitting on the passenger seat, contemplating whether he should share the story of his new patient with Abbey. It still weighed heavily on his mind.

Abbey had retired just a week before their vacation in the Bahamas, and although she had expressed interest in his work, he believed it was too soon to burden her with these disturbing details. She deserved a peaceful and restful retirement, and he couldn't bear to disrupt her tranquility. She had encouraged him to follow suit and retire, but even at seventy, he couldn't envision himself giving up the profession he loved. He believed he still had valuable years left in him to make a difference.

The curtains in the front room parted, and Abbey's smile warmly welcomed him. Her silhouette bathed in the gentle light from their home. Holding a glass of wine, she beckoned him inside.

Allen grinned and waved back, his heart filled with love and contentment. Abbey remained the most beautiful woman in the world, and her presence in the window confirmed his happiness. He truly believed he was the luckiest man on earth.

Allen hurried to the passenger side of his car, clutching the box, and entered their home. Abbey was waiting for him, and she greeted him with a kiss.

"What do you have there?" she inquired.

"Oh, it's nothing," Allen replied nonchalantly. "Just a case file on a new patient, a kid named Zackary Williams." With the box in hand, he headed toward his office. Glancing back at Abbey, he noticed the puzzled expression on her face.

Sensing her curiosity, he asked, "Is something bothering you, Abbey?"

Abbey forced a smile, clearly wrestling with her thoughts. "No, I'm sorry. Everything is fine. I'm just curious about why the state is placing Williams at Churchill. I thought they were committing him to Patton State Hospital in California."

Allen paused, pondering her question, a thoughtful expression on his face. The mystery of Zackary Williams and the unexplained choice of Churchill over Patton State Hospital lingered in the air, a question mark in an already perplexing case.

Allen moved closer to Abbey, his expression serious as he delved into the conversation about the Williams case.

"So you're familiar with the Williams case?" he asked.

Abbey shrugged, her gaze distant as she recalled the limited details she had gathered. "A little while ago, I talked to an old colleague who works at Running Springs. She had little to say on the matter, only that Williams had murdered his parents with an ax, and law enforcement had discovered multiple other bodies on the property." Abbey paused and met Allen's eyes. "I presume you will go through his case file?"

Allen nodded, confirming her assumption. "Yes, I always do before placement."

The gruesome nature of the case weighed heavily on their conversation, and Allen was tempted to ask why Abbey had never mentioned it to him before. However, he understood that it had seemed irrelevant to their lives until now.

"Anyway, Williams is being transported to Churchill in the morning. I'll let you know how it goes when I get home. Why don't we let it go tonight, okay?" Allen suggested, hoping to shift the focus away from the grim topic.

Abbey agreed, offering a smile. "Okay, no more work discussions tonight. I'll save all my questions for tomorrow." She sipped her wine, and the couple decided to set aside the unsettling case for the evening and embrace the comfort of their shared moments together.

Down The Rabbit Hole

The following morning, Dr. Allen Creed entered his office at Churchill Hospital. Unlike his sterile, nondescript office at Ridge Rock, his workspace at Churchill exuded warmth and character. He had filled the dark wooden bookshelves with books by his favorite authors—John Steinbeck, J. R. R. Tolkien, and Stephen King. Additionally, he had amassed hundreds of medical journals and criminal law books, their spines stretching from floor to ceiling.

As Allen took in the familiar surroundings, he couldn't help but feel a sense of nervous anticipation. However, he knew it was time to face the inevitable and meet his new patient. He had to make the call and begin the process.

Fifteen minutes later, a soft knock echoed at his door, followed by the voice of a Corrections officer.

"Dr. Creed, I have Mr. Williams here."

Allen stepped away from his desk and opened the door. Before him sat Zackary Williams, securely shackled by his wrists and ankles to a blue wheelchair. Allen's initial impression was of the young man's imposing size. He wore state-issued orange coveralls and brown sandals. His shoulders were broad, his scarred hands massive, and his physique lean. Yet, despite his imposing appearance, Zackary appeared frozen in place, much like a frightened child, his gaze fixed motionless

22

on his lap. Scars on the recently shaved head served as a grim reminder of the severe abuse he had endured throughout his life.

Greeting the young man, Allen extended a welcoming hand. "Good morning, Mr. Williams. My name is Dr. Creed."

However, Zackary remained unresponsive, his silence looming heavily in the room.

Officer Woods cleared his throat, breaking the tension in the room. "He doesn't say much, Dr. Creed. He does what we tell him to do, no less, no more."

Dr. Creed acknowledged Woods with a nod. "Thank you, Officer. You can wait outside."

As Officer Woods left the room, Allen adjusted Zackary's chair and sat across from him.

"Mr. Williams, I want to start by telling you how pleased I am to meet you. As you may or may not know, I will be your psychiatrist during your stay here. Therefore, everything we discuss will remain between you and me. Do you understand, Mr. Williams?"

Zackary's response was a hesitant shrug, but he found solace in the kindness of Dr. Creed's voice. It was a stark contrast to the torment he had endured from his parents, who seemed to revel in taunting him even in death.

"My name is Zackary, not Mr. Williams," he rasped, his voice strained. Almost immediately, he heard the mocking laughter of his parents from behind him. It was a reminder that they were never too far away, and they seemed to enjoy tormenting him whenever they could.

Killing them had not silenced them; if anything, it made their presence more haunting.

Dr. Creed intervened, attempting to maintain the conversation.

"Well, we are off to a wonderful start, Zackary," he remarked, showing understanding and patience.

Zackary remained silent, his reluctance to engage stemming from the fear that responding to Dr. Creed might lead to further torment from his parents.

Noticing Zackary's discomfort, Dr. Creed leaned back in his chair and spoke gently. "Zackary, we have plenty of time. Take as long as you like. When you are ready to talk, we will begin."

Zackary listened but was still apprehensive about speaking. He knew his parents were lurking behind him, and their silence was ominous. There was a slow, rhythmic tapping sound that added to his unease. Unable to resist any longer, he turned to look over his right shoulder, and what he saw confirmed his worst fears. His parents staring at him, their expressions pained. And both were still clad in the same bloodstained clothes they had worn the night he killed them.

Zackary's father draped his left arm around the shoulders of his sobbing mother. She looked down, cradling a gaping wound in her abdomen. From the horrific gash, blood trickled in streams down her nightgown before dripping onto the floor with a tap-tapping sound. Zackary turned his head away, squeezing his eyes closed. Although he could block the image of his parents, the sound of his father's voice tormented him.

"Zack, you pile of shit. Turn around and look at what you did to us. We can't stop bleeding. You hurt us real bad, son. Your momma doesn't stop crying because of what you did to her. She's hurting, and there ain't nothing anyone can do to fix it."

The words reverberated in Zackary's mind, creating a cacophony of guilt and despair. His actions had not brought the peace he had hoped for; instead, they had bound him to a never-ending nightmare with his vengeful, tormented parents.

Zackary's father's enraged voice, as well as his mother's sobbing, rose to an ear-piercing volume. "Don't ignore me, boy. Turn around and look at what you did to your—" His father abruptly went silent.

It was Jacob; from somewhere down the hall, he whistled a cheerful, obscure melody. As he approached the room, he called out, "Zackary, oh Zackary, come out, come out wherever you are."

Zackary grinned. He knew Jacob was aware of exactly where he was. Jacob was playing games with his parents; they were terrified of him and fled in panic whenever Jacob was near, and he was very near. Jacob gently tapped on the office door.

"Oh, Zackary, I think I found you, and by the sound of things, you have company. Is that Momma and Daddy in there?" The atmosphere in the room grew heavy and oppressive as Jacob's presence drew nearer. Zackary's parents had gone eerily silent, and their fear was palpable. The blood tapping on the floor quickened, and Zackary felt like he was on the precipice of something terrible. The impending storm of fear and anxiety was almost suffocating.

Outside Allen's office, Officer Woods looked up from his newspaper. For a fleeting moment, he sensed a disturbance. A little red flag deep within his subconsciousness fluttered before returning to its placid state. Woods glanced down both ends of the hallway before shrugging it off and returning to the sports page.

Zackary stared at the door. The doorknob slowly twisted before returning to its position. Zackary nervously glanced at Allen before returning his attention to the door.

The door softly creaked before Jacob melted through it and into the room. Jacob grinned as he waved to Zackary. Zackary was so overwhelmed he forgot he was shackled by his wrists to the arms of the wheelchair. When he tried to wave, he jerked the chair, shifting it sideways. Zackary quickly turned, glancing at Allen.

"I'm sorry about that. I just had a back spasm."

Allen chuckled. "That's all right, Zackary. I get those all the time."

Zackary forced a smile before looking back toward Jacob.

"I'm here now, Zack," he said before turning a heated gaze toward Zackary's parents. "Both of you leave this room before I do something you won't like."

They stared wide-eyed at him, frozen in terror. Jacob yelled, "NOW!"

Zackary's parents recoiled at Jacob's command and scrambled to leave the room. They moved quickly, fear etched on their spectral faces, as they crossed the room, leaving a ragged trail of blood in their wake.

Zackary watched in awe as his parents dissipated through the door, their ominous presence fading into the shadows. He turned his gaze upward, where Jacob stood with a warm, reassuring smile.

"Where have you been all day?" Zackary questioned, a hint of concern in his voice. "I was afraid you couldn't find me."

Jacob gently patted Zackary's shoulder, his touch a comforting reassurance. "I always know where you are. Just because you can't see me doesn't mean I'm not nearby."

Zackary's brow furrowed with a mixture of emotions. "I know," he began, his voice tinged with vulnerability. "I was just getting a little worried. You've been staying away longer and longer. I hardly see you anymore. It hurts my feelings."

Jacob's eyes twinkled with understanding, his grin warm and caring. "Well, don't get yourself worked up over nothing," he advised. "Now, listen to me, Zack. You need to talk to Dr. Creed. You need to tell him everything that happened while we lived at home."

Zackary's hesitation was palpable, his fear evident. "I don't want to," he admitted, his voice quivering. "I'm scared. You know I don't talk to anyone else except for you."

Despite the daunting nature of the situation, Jacob's voice remained tender yet resolute. "Well, you're going to talk to Dr. Creed, and you're going to start right now."

Meanwhile, Allen quietly observed Zackary's conversation with Jacob in the background. To an outsider, it appeared to be a one-sided dialogue with an unseen entity, but Allen knew better. He recognized that Zackary was communicating with someone or something very real to him, a presence that provided him with comfort and guidance.

Finally, Zackary glanced anxiously at Allen and then back at Jacob. In a hushed whisper, he mustered the courage to say, "Okay, I'll do it. I'll tell him everything."

Zackary took comfort in Jacob's presence and was gradually opening up to the idea of speaking to Dr. Creed. He glanced over at Allen, his gaze now more focused, his demeanor less hesitant.

"Jacob wants me to tell you my story," Zackary explained. He nodded toward Jacob, who had seated himself cross-legged on the floor, displaying an eager curiosity.

Allen maintained a warm and empathetic demeanor. "Tell me about Jacob, Zackary. Who is he?"

Zackary's voice held a sense of respect and camaraderie. "Jacob is my twin, except he's smarter than me. So he goes everywhere with me. He can be a little irritating sometimes when he gives me advice, but he's usually right."

Allen couldn't help but feel intrigued by this dynamic. "Well, as long as he gives you good advice and not the kind that would cause you or anyone else any harm."

Zackary reassured him, "Oh, it's never terrible advice. It's always the kind that ends up helping me out

Allen's grin conveyed his approval. "Well, that sounds fine, Zackary." He then pointed out the recording equipment in the room. "Zackary, as you know, you have been accused of doing some terrible things. This situation requires me to record everything we discuss in this room. You should also know that there is a small camera behind me on the wall. These things are here to protect you." Allen's tone was gentle and reassuring. "Do you understand everything I've told you, Zackary?"

Zackary nodded. "I understand, Doctor. I don't think Jacob would ask me to talk to you if he thought you were a bad person.

"Zackary, I'm glad you understand. You seem like a reasonable young man, and you're right; I'm not a bad person. You're here with me only to ensure you receive the proper help you deserve."

Zackary noticed Dr. Creed had picked up a silver pen and written something on his notepad. He was sure it had something to do with his willingness to cooperate.

"Zackary, before we begin, would you like me to get you a cup of water?"

Zackary smirked, "No, Doctor. I just want to get this done."

Allen smiled. "What do you mean by getting this done?"

Zackary smirked. "Doctor, please, no dumb-ass questions. I just want to tell you my story and be done with it. That's all I meant. I want to get this part of my life over so I can get out of this chair and into a room, cell, or whatever they have planned for me. I'm sick and tired of people asking me questions." Again, Zack noticed Dr. Creed write something on the notepad.

Allen looked up at Zackary. "Okay, Zackary, fair enough. We'll begin whenever you are ready. I'll try not to interrupt you, but I must warn you I'm inquisitive. I may ask a few questions, but it's my nature to do so. It drives my wife up the wall.

Zackary chuckled. "All right, I suppose I can handle a few questions." Zackary cleared his throat. "Doctor, do you mind if I face the other way while I talk to you? I'd feel better if I didn't have to look at you while telling my life story. I know that sounds crazy, but it would make me feel a whole hell of a lot better."

More writing on the notepad. Allen stood from his chair and walked around the desk. He was smiling as if conversing with a man shackled to a wheelchair was the most common thing in the world to him. In Allen's profession, it was.

Allen turned Zackary around to face the door, then locked the brakes on the wheels.

That struck Zackary as a little peculiar, considering his wrists were shackled to the chair's armrest.

Allen patted Zackary's back as he strolled back to his desk. Zackary did not recoil or attempt to pull away from a gesture of kindness, a positive sign Allen thought.

"Zackary, I understand I said I wouldn't ask too many questions, but for the record, I must ask a few basic questions for documentation. Will that be okay?

"I guess." Zackary heard the pen scratch on the paper.

"Okay, so tell me your full name," Allen said.

"Zackary Charles Williams," Zackary replied.

"When were you born, Zackary?"

"I was born on August 7, 1987."

"How old are you?"

"Eighteen."

"Do you know what day of the week it is?"

Zackary thought. He hadn't kept track of the days of the week in months. "I'm not sure," he replied nervously.

The pen scratched.

"What month is it, Zackary?" Zackary thought again.

"Sorry, not sure about that either."

Scratching. "What year is it, Zackary?"

Zackary felt uneasy; he feared Dr. Creed would be angry if he kept answering his questions wrong.

Zackary looked down at his lap. "Doctor, I'm sorry I don't remember. I'm a little shaken up."

The pen scratched. "That's okay, Zackary. I'm almost finished with the preliminary questions." "Good, I'd just like to get started."

Allen set his pen down before glancing at his recorder, its green light indicating it was on. It was time to delve into the mind of a twisted mind.

"Whenever you are ready, you can start Zachary."

Zackary shrugged. "I've done a lot of bad things. The worst thing is I killed my momma and daddy."

Allen cleared his throat. "Okay, Zackary, would you mind telling me about that and what led to you killing your parents?"

Zackary didn't respond.

Allen observed Zackary's physical reaction to the mention of the most significant and painful event in his life. The young man's fear and emotional distress were evident, with his shoulders rising and falling as he struggled to find the words. Allen knew Zackary was frightened. However, he needed to remain calm. Otherwise, he feared Zackary would again close himself off to the world.

Allen interrupted the silence. "Take your time, Zackary. We have all day. Just ask if you want to take a break during our session."

Zackary glanced over his shoulder at Allen. "I don't need any breaks. I'm just going to start talking now."

"Well, if you want my entire life story, it starts like this. Like I said, I was born in August of '87. My momma, Darleen, and my daddy, Charlie, were pretty young when I came into their lives. I think Momma was only sixteen, and Daddy was around nineteen. Anyway, we lived in the same house all my life until I made a mess of the place. Before that, it was spotless. Momma was some kind of neat freak. She was always cleaning the inside of our house. I thought it was funny, especially considering the outside looked like shit. The paint was peeling off the walls, and Daddy and Grandpa scattered cars all over the yard. It looked like a fucking junkyard. I bet it still does, but it was home to her, I guess."

"The house sat right smack in the middle of three hundred acres of land, which Grandpa said had been in the family for over a hundred years. Growing up there was usually peaceful. We pretty much did whatever we wanted."

Allen interrupted. "Zackary, you said it was usually peaceful. What did you mean by that?"

Zackary shrugged, "Well, from time to time, we had run-ins with, let's just say, things that wouldn't make much sense to the average person.

"What things?" Allen asked.

Zackary sighed; Allen's interruptions were beginning to rouse an anger that Zack didn't want to surface. "Let's just leave it at that for now."

"Okay, Zackary, I'll let you set the pace. Then, when you are ready, we can get back to that. You mentioned you did pretty much whatever you wanted out there. What things?"

Zackary grinned, thinking, "Oh, Doctor, if you only knew."

"Mostly hunting. Daddy and Grandpa always took me along whenever they went. I loved going with them. It made me feel important, like a man, not just some snot-nosed kid. Now and again, we would stay out overnight in an old cabin Grandpa built out of wood, Grandpa chopped himself. It wasn't much, but it served its purpose."

Intrigued, Allen asked, "What kind of purpose, Zack?"

Zackary pondered how to address. He would have never told Dr. Creed or anyone else about what took place in the cabin if Jacob hadn't told him to.

"Okay, Doctor, this is going to sound like Daddy and Grandpa were crazy, but sometimes they had a girlfriend wait out in the cabin for them. Of course, they didn't allow me to go in when they did their business, but I knew what was happening. It sounded like Daddy and Grandpa were having a hell of a good time, if you know what I mean."

"Did your mom or grandma know about the lady friends, Zackary?"

Zack laughed. "Are you crazy? My momma would've killed both Daddy and Grandpa. She wouldn't have put up with that shit, and as far as Grandma is concerned, I never knew her. She died long before I was born."

"So you never went into the cabin when the ladies were there?"

"No, as I said, they didn't allow me to see them, but I did have to clean up after them. Those ladies would leave a hell of a mess. There were times when I found blood all over the walls and floors. I asked Daddy once why there was so much blood everywhere. Daddy told me they were just some crazy bitches who loved to drink and get the shit kicked out of them. I never believed him, though. I mean, who the hell wants to have the crap kicked out of them? I thought it was strange. I never saw the ladies leave. When I asked Daddy about that, he told me the ladies usually left really late when I was sleeping. He told me they had night jobs and had to go home before their husbands knew they were out messing around. Looking back now, I know Daddy and Grandpa were killing those ladies, but I wasn't old enough to know any better at the time."

"We always went home the next day as if nothing happened. Momma never asked questions. I guess she figured she didn't have any business asking about men's affairs."

"We had a lot of good times and, of course, a lot of bad times at that old house. One of the worst nights of my life happened when I was seven years old; I was lying in bed, listening to the rain smacking hard on our old tin roof like a jackhammer. I liked the sound of that. It made my bed feel cozy, knowing I was safe and warm and not out in the weather. There were no lights in my bedroom except my Darth Vader night light. I hated that goddamn thing. It scared the shit out of me. It made spooky shadows on the walls and ceiling that seemed to have a life of their own. I couldn't understand why any kid would want that damn thing in their room."

"Anyway, I heard a lot of bumping around downstairs and my momma yelling. Of course, I couldn't hear everything she was saying, but I could tell by her voice that whatever was going on, it pissed her off. So, being curious, I crawled out of bed and tiptoed to the door so I could listen in better."

"Momma was yelling something about someone being inside the house. I wasn't sure what the hell she was talking about, so I peeked out my door to see what was happening downstairs. I remember seeing Momma run from the kitchen door toward a woman lying at the top of the cellar stairs. Momma shoved Grandpa out of her way, then took hold of that lady's hair before throwing her backward down the steps. That was enough for me. I didn't want to see anymore. I ran back to my bed, jumped under my blankets, and covered my head with my pillow. I tried blocking out all the noise going on downstairs, but that didn't work out too well.

All Things Must Come to an End

Twenty-three-year-old Elizabeth Tooler sat at her favorite spot, a heavily graffiti-covered bus stop with a single bench. However, it had been many years since a bus stopped there. Someone shot and killed the last driver who braved the route during a botched robbery attempt.

The incident spelled the end of public transportation for the entire area, including private taxi companies and all package delivery services. The few people who ventured onto Mill Street after dark seldom left unscathed. It was a well-known fact by those unfortunate enough to live in the third-world-style apartments lining Mill Street - don't bother calling 911 after dark; no one was showing up.

Elizabeth felt right at home. Years of narcotic abuse and narcotic-induced mental illness desensitized her to the danger. To her, it was home, and she liked it. But it wasn't always that way. She had many close friends in her not-so-distant past, and each once regarded her as a stunning young woman living the perfect life.

Her doting parents were physicians who raised her in an upper-middle-class neighborhood. They had provided her with everything she desired. She excelled in school, and with her academic accomplishments came several scholarships to prestigious universities. Her future was full of promise, but it ended at a high school graduation party. A single powdery white rail on a methamphetamine-dusted mirror was all it took.

Elizabeth glanced down at her feet. The roving transients had missed a half-smoked cigarette. "Score," she thought before plucking it up and lighting the lipstick-stained cigarette. She inhaled deeply, relishing the subtle burn at the back of her throat before exhaling a large plume of rancid smoke. It was going to be a great night.

Elizabeth took a final drag of the gritty cigarette before carelessly flicking it into the street. She glanced down the street, noticing yellowish headlights gradually approaching. Instead of driving past her, the deteriorating early-model pickup truck squealed to a stop at the trash-littered curb in front of her. The truck's engine throbbed as it struggled to run, belching blue smoke from its rusted tailpipe.

Elizabeth squinted as she tried to see the driver. From inside the darkness of the cab, a pale hand extended toward her, waving a fistful of cash.

A man with a gruff voice asked, "Are you working, hon?"

Elizabeth grinned, "Depends on what you have in mind and how much you're willing to pay," she said.

"I've got two hundred bucks right here." The man extended his arm a little closer to the open passenger window. "That should be more than enough to start this little party."

Two hundred bucks? Elizabeth's eyes narrowed; something wasn't right; fifty bucks would have been excessive, and two hundred was ridiculous. The little voice in the back of her mind raised the alarm; something wasn't right here.

"What's your name, mister?" she asked.

"Not that it fucking matters, but you can call me Charlie."

It mattered; too many things could and had gone wrong in her line of work. The word on the streets spread quickly, and at least she would now have a name—presumably not a real one, but it was something.

As she opened the passenger door, she hesitated; the little voice inside her head was screaming, "Don't do this," Before deciding whether to enter the truck, Charlie grabbed her hand, forcefully pulling her inside his lair.

Elizabeth's head smashed onto the steering wheel, stunned; she caught a glimpse of her assailant's hideous face as she collapsed onto Charlie's lap. There was no time to defend herself before he began pummeling her, sending her into the void of darkness.

Elizabeth's consciousness slowly rekindled, unraveling the tangled tapestry of the night's harrowing events into a semblance of order. She recollected the grotesque visage of the man, the merciless assault that ensued, and the unsettling sway of the truck as she lay sprawled amidst discarded debris on the floorboard. Her mind's eye flickered with the memory of a furtive glance shared with the man, who, in turn, had noticed her stirring and responded with a vicious, bone-shattering blow to her face, plunging her back into the abyss of unconsciousness.

Lying on an unforgivingly frigid surface, Elizabeth's senses gradually returned to her. Faint voices reached her ears, their cadence muffled.

With immense effort, Elizabeth forced her swollen eyes open. Her vision remained blurred, but it revealed her grim surroundings. She lay on the cold, damp concrete floor of a pitch-black cellar. Every movement sent sharp pains radiating through her battered body, but she managed to prop herself up against the clammy wall.

Her gaze wandered through the darkness and discerned the bleak truth: she was confined in a decrepit cellar. Opposite her, a dim outline showed a rickety staircase ascending to a pair of imposing double doors, firmly sealed with a heavy chain lock.

Beside the stairs leading up, a second set of steps beckoned, their warped surfaces catching feeble glimmers from the lights filtering down from the residence above. Elizabeth, determined to escape this dismal cellar, summoned all her remaining strength.

With every step sending jolts of pain coursing through Elizabeth's battered frame, she rose, using the wall for support. Clinging to hope, she shuffled toward the uneven staircase, her fingers trembling but her spirit resolute.

Raising her gaze, she found herself confronted by an elderly figure, his silvery beard cascading like a waterfall, clad in worn and tattered overalls. His blank stare fixated upon her from the stairway above. Unlike the brute who had inflicted brutal violence upon her, this old man bore no semblance of madness; instead, he emanated the air of a bewildered, elderly soul.

Elizabeth didn't know who he was or why he was there, but she saw a chance to escape.

Elizabeth's heart raced, knowing that if Charlie returned, her life hung by a thread. She couldn't afford to waste any time. Gritting her teeth against the pain, she began to crawl painstakingly up the short flight of stairs, the old man at the top remaining motionless and unresponsive.

Reaching the top of the stairs, she pleaded hoarsely, "Please, mister. I need your help; I'll do anything. My name is Elizabeth, Elizabeth Tooler. If you need money, my parents will give it to you." Her voice quivered with a mixture of desperation and hope.

However, the old man didn't react to her words, continuing to glare as if her desperate plea meant nothing. Undeterred, Elizabeth grasped his pant leg, urging, "Mister, all you have to do is help me get out of here, and then I'll leave. You'll never see me again. I won't tell anyone—"

Her sentence was cut short as Darleen, dressed in a tattered white nightgown, entered the room with Charlie close behind. The dim light cast eerie shadows on their contorted faces, making them look like specters from a nightmare.

Spotting Elizabeth, Darleen became furious, screaming. "Daddy, it's in the house. It's in the fucking house!" She then turned her attention back to Elizabeth, demanding action. "Did you hear me, Daddy? It's in the fucking house. Do something!"

Charlie hesitated, and before he could react, Darleen rushed past him, pushing Grandpa aside, and headed straight for Elizabeth. With a burst of violence, she gripped Elizabeth's hair firmly with both hands, leaving her helpless to defend herself.

In a brutal motion, Darleen threw Elizabeth into the cellar's depths.

As Elizabeth tumbled down the stairs, everything seemed to slow down before she landed with a jolt on the cold concrete floor below.

Miraculously, Elizabeth remained conscious. "Good," she thought, grateful that she could at least put up some resistance. However, she knew better than to crawl back up the stairs and back into the clutches of the maniacs. That would be a fatal mistake. For now, she lay still, hoping they would believe her to be unconscious or even dead.

From above, Darleen's yelling still reached her ears, fueling her fear and determination to find a way out.

Darleen turned and faced Charlie, struggling to catch her breath. "I told you not to let it get into the house," she said with frustration. "And, Grandpa, what the fuck were you doing just standing there watching her?"

Charlie walked past Darleen, heading toward the cellar. "I'm sorry, momma, it won't ever happen again."

"And what about you, Grandpa?" she asked as he followed Charlie down the stairs. Without glancing back, he flatly responded, "I'm sorry."

When Grandpa reached Elizabeth, he knelt and tenderly lifted her off the floor, carrying her limp body toward the bathtub. The scene played out like some macabre theater production in the dimly lit, decaying cellar.

Meanwhile, Charlie was getting ready, slipping into a rubber apron, adding a surreal touch to the twisted performance.

With an eerie gentleness, Grandpa set Elizabeth down beside the old clawfoot tub. His trembling hands struggled to guide her head toward it, creating a chilling tableau in the dim cellar. In a heart-stopping instant, Elizabeth's eyes fluttered open, only to be met by Charlie's cold, steel gaze and the glint of a large knife pressed against her throat. Her terrified screams echoed in the underground chamber as she fought desperately to break free from Grandpa's unyielding grasp.

Summoning the very depths of her terror, Elizabeth unleashed a final, desperate struggle. Her nails raked across Grandpa's face, eliciting a tortured scream from him as he released his grip, staggering back in pain. Blood poured from his injured eyes, his hands now clutching his wounded face.

Elizabeth's adrenaline-fueled determination gave her a burst of agility. She narrowly avoided Charlie's grasping hands, rolling free and causing him to lose his balance. He crashed into the wall, disoriented and furious. Through clenched teeth, he hissed, "I'm gonna fucking kill you, bitch."

Elizabeth's foot collided with a small table by the tub in her frantic scramble, sending a red toolbox tumbling to the floor, its contents scattering like the remains of a broken dream. Panicking, she reached for the nearest object she could grasp—a small paring knife gleaming in the dim light.

With a swift, covert movement, Elizabeth clutched the knife and slid backward, inching closer to the safety of the stairs. Bewildered by the unexpected twist, Charlie advanced hesitantly, his focus torn between her and Grandpa, whose moans echoed through the room, his hand clamped over the injured eye.

Elizabeth positioned herself at the foot of the stairs, her back pressed firmly against the wall. She was determined not to let either of them gain an advantage by getting behind her.

With a wild, feral snarl, Grandpa launched himself at Elizabeth, clawing and snapping, his old frame moving with surprising aggression.

Elizabeth frantically slashed at his throat, finding her mark. Blood splattered her face as Grandpa fell, clutching his throat to the floor. With Grandpa no longer a threat, she turned her attention to Charlie. She pointed the knife at him.

Elizabeth screamed, "Get back! Get away from me, you sick fucking bastard."

Charlie's eyes blazed with rage as he lunged at her, wildly slashing his knife. Elizabeth felt the searing sting of the blade as it slammed into her chest. Desperate, she attempted to kick free, but she was outmatched.

Charlie swiftly pinned her arms down at her side with his knees before stabbing fiercely into her chest. As Elizabeth's life's blood poured from her body onto the floor, she could no longer grip the knife. She looked up at the spider web-covered ceiling and watched it fade into darkness.

War Paint

"I wasn't hiding in my bed for too long before I went downstairs to see what was happening. I found Momma sitting on the couch. She was crying," Zackary recounted, reflecting on the disturbing events. "I asked her, 'Momma, what's going on with that lady?'"

He continued, "I scared the hell out of momma. She damn near flew off the couch. I thought she knew I was standing beside her, but I was wrong. She grabbed hold of me and held me real tight. I could tell whatever was happening; it shook her up."

"Oh, hon, it's nothing. Your daddy caught a hog out in the yard. He thought he knocked it out before dragging it into the cellar, but I guess it came to and started up the stairs,"

"I was so damned confused, so I said, "I didn't see a hog. What I saw was a lady." Zackary laughed, "That pissed Momma off.""

"Listen, there ain't no ladies in this house except me. What you saw was a hog. Now run your ass upstairs and go back to bed," she yelled.

"I was afraid to argue about it anymore, but when I started walking toward the stairs. The noise from the cellar got louder; I looked at Momma. What are they doing down there? Why is that hog making so much noise?"

Momma had it, she started yelling. "Run your ass up those stairs right now."

"Momma ran up the stairs right behind me. Then it came, the awful sound of Grandpa yelling all gurgle-like like he was holding his head underwater and trying to talk. The next thing I saw was Daddy stumbling up the basement stairs covered in blood, with Grandpa staggering behind him. Grandpa was holding both of his hands around his throat. I'll never get the sight of that out of my head. Blood was spraying through his fingers like a hose getting all over the place,"

"Daddy yelled at Momma, 'Get a towel. Get a goddamn fucking towel!' Momma just stood there. I guess she was too scared to do anything. So I ran to the kitchen and grabbed Momma's favorite dish towel from the oven door. Funny how you remember such stupid shit like that, but I can still see that damn sunflower towel wrapped around Grandpa's throat as he lay at the top of the cellar stairs."

"That flower went from bright yellow to red in seconds. You wouldn't think so, but I remember thinking I would get strapped for grabbing Momma's favorite towel. But I figured that would come when it did. For the time being, we had to save Grandpa's life."

"I knelt beside Grandpa to help Daddy put pressure on the cut. Daddy was having a hell of a time because Grandpa was thrashing around like a fish out of water. He was kicking his legs in every direction, grabbing hold of Daddy and me, and scratching at us all crazy like he was a wildcat. He got the side of my face pretty good, too. I didn't get mad though. He was hurting a lot, and I knew it. I remember he was trying to say something, but his mouth was frothy, so we couldn't understand a word. It sounded more like he was growling than anything else."

"I'll never forget the look in his eyes either. They were darting all over the place like he was searching for something. I could tell he wasn't ready to go yet, but that cut was too deep, and there was nothing we could do to stop the bleeding."

"It didn't take long before Grandpa went limp and passed on into heaven. But I'll tell you, I was happy about it. I was tired of holding him down while getting the shit kicked out of me."

"Things were almost like a dream after he finally died. First, I remember everything going so quiet that I could hear the crickets chirping outside. After a while, Daddy and I just stared at him. I don't think it sunk in that he was gone yet. Honestly, I was more worried about the mess he left on the floor and all over Momma's good towel."

"I looked up at Momma. She was still standing by the couch. She had one hand over her mouth and the other pointed downstairs. I looked back to see what she was looking at, and goddamn, if that hog wasn't crawling back up the stairs. She was dragging her legs behind her, but all the same, she was heading straight toward us. I just kind of froze up. I tried to run, but my legs wouldn't move."

"Daddy must've frozen up, too, because he wasn't doing anything but watching. But I'll be honest, what scared me the most was no matter what Momma had told me earlier, she didn't look like a hog to me."

Allen cleared his throat before asking, "What did she look like, Zackary?"

Zackary thought for a moment. If he went further with his story, he would have to tell certain things that were supposed to be family secrets, but Jacob had told him to tell his story, but did he mean everything? Even his darkest secrets?

Allen sat quietly. Zackary's head slowly turned from side to side as if he were in deep thought.

Allen pressed Zackary for an answer, "Zackary, can you please tell me what the thing coming up the stairs looked like? It's okay. You can tell me, Zack. You're in a safe place. Remember what I told you earlier? Everything you tell me can only help you and your case. I'm your friend, Zack. You can tell me anything."

Zackary whispered, "Jacob, what do you want me to say?"

Jacob rolled his eyes. "Tell him everything, Zack, don't hide nothing; I have a plan."

"Zackary, are you talking to Jacob?" asked Allen.

Zackary nodded. "Yes, Doctor, we were just having a little talk."

Pen scratching.

Zackary continued, "So anyway, here she comes, real slow-like, and she was staring right at me. She must have had charcoal or something around her eyes because it was all streaked down her cheeks. She looked like she was wearing war paint or something. I remember her having long brown hair, all thrown this way and that like she'd been rolling around. I never saw a hog with long hair like that. At least not before that day. She scared the shit out of me."

"Then here's the crazy part. She started talking to me. She did, Doctor. She said, 'Help me. Please help me' or something along those lines. I started screaming as loud as I could. I tried standing up to run to Momma but kept slipping in Grandpa's blood. So I started kicking and sliding backward until Momma got hold of me. She picked me up and started running up the stairs while yelling at Daddy."

"She howled, 'Kill her, Daddy. Kill her before she gets up in the house again.' "Just as we reached the top of the stairs, I looked over Momma's shoulder and saw Daddy grab that hog by its hair and throw her down the stairs. Then, before Momma closed my bedroom door, I saw Daddy grab that nasty hog by the hair again and drag her around the corner. There was a second or two of a real loud squealing. Then it was quiet."

"Both me and Momma looked at each other. Neither one of us was sure what was happening downstairs. Then Momma walked to my door and opened it. She yelled down the stairs, 'Daddy, are you okay?' "I heard Daddy answer from the cellar. 'I'm all right. The bitch is dead.' "Momma walked over to my bed and told me to sleep."

Zackary shook his head, "Can you believe that? She told me to get some sleep."

"I told Momma, 'Momma, I don't think I can."

"She wasn't having that though, she said," "Now you listen, boy. You do what I tell you. You stay up here and go to sleep."

"It scared me to death. How could any kid just go to sleep after seeing all that? But I wasn't going to argue, so I just told her I'd try. Momma wrapped her arms around me and sang Jesus loves me until I fell asleep. It took a long time; I was still pretty shaken up."

Zackary continued, recollecting, "I woke up late the next day. The rain had stopped, and the sun was shining into my room. It was nice out. I just lay in bed for a while, thinking about the night before and hoping it was all a dream, but I knew it wasn't. So I got up, got myself dressed, and then went downstairs."

"Momma had cleaned up most of Grandpa's blood, except for the basement stairs. They were permanently stained black."

"I could hear Momma singing in the kitchen while the house smelled of delicious food. She was cooking my favorite, bacon and eggs. Her cooking was the best I've ever had." Zackary paused, recalling his moms home home-cooked meals. "Anyway, I walked into the kitchen, expecting Momma to say something about her towel, but she didn't mention it. Instead, she turned around from the stove, spatula in hand, and acted as if nothing had happened the night before. She said, 'Morning, baby doll, are you hungry?'"

"I shrugged, still worrying about that towel. 'Yes, Momma.'"

"Well, sit at the table, and I'll get you some breakfast. It's just about done.' Momma smiled and patted me on my rear as I walked past her toward the table."

"Momma, where's Daddy?" I asked.

"Well, baby, Daddy's just finishing up in the basement with that ornery hog from last night. He'll be right up.'"

"Then I asked, 'Momma, how did Grandpa get cut last night?'"

"Momma froze for a moment, not turning around from the stove. 'It was an accident. Daddy said your grandpa got too close to that hog, and it bit his throat out.'"

"I pondered on that for a minute or two. Then I remember thinking, 'Goddamn, it bit his throat out. Where's Grandpa now?'"

"'Well, baby, for now, we're going to keep Grandpa in the freezer downstairs. Daddy says it's too muddy to lay Grandpa in the ground. He wants to wait till it dries up a bit.'"

"I thought that sounded strange, but Daddy always knew best. I knew I shouldn't ask about grown-up things, but I took a chance with my next question. 'What did Daddy do about that lady?'"

"Momma put my breakfast on the table and sat beside me. She looked at me as if I were crazy. 'What lady are you talking about?'"

"The lady from last night, Momma, the one I heard asking Daddy to let her go."

"Momma smiled. 'Oh, don't you worry about that hog. She ain't ever gonna be coming around here again.'"

"Of course, I wasn't satisfied with that answer. 'I didn't ask about a hog. I asked about that lady. 'You said Daddy caught that hog in the yard. Why was it in the yard, Momma?'"

"Momma was getting a little tired of all my questions, so she just said, 'Why don't you shut your damn mouth and eat your breakfast?'"

"I knew I was pushing my luck, but I asked, 'Momma, can I talk to you about one more thing?'"

"Momma kind of sighed and said, 'Well, go ahead, boy. One more thing, and that's it.'"

"I wasn't sure how to ask my next question, so I just said, 'Momma, you know that hog Daddy and Grandpa were killing?'"

"Yes, baby.'"

"Well, when it came crawling up the stairs last night, it didn't look like a hog. It kind of looked like a person. Like a lady or something."

"Momma smiled again. 'Honey, sometimes a child's imagination can get mixed up when something horrible happens. What you saw was nothing but an old sow. That's all, sweetie. Your mind was just trying too hard to figure things out. Now you eat your breakfast. Your daddy's going to need your help later.'"

Zackary continued, "I knew better than to ask any more questions after that. I finished breakfast and waited on the porch for Daddy. After a few minutes, he came out with a cup of coffee and sat beside me. I could tell he was upset, so I figured I ought to say something. 'Daddy, Momma says you need help with something later.'"

"Daddy looked down at me and smiled. 'That's right, boy.' Daddy took a sip of his coffee and then stared straight ahead. I asked him what he needed help with. 'We're gonna take some things to the pond.'"

"Daddy nodded straight ahead, so I knew which one he meant. We had three ponds. The one straight through the woods Daddy and Grandpa called the pig pond. It was where they would throw out all the guts and stuff left over from the hog. They never allowed me to go to that one alone, but I always wanted to."

"Sometimes around dusk, Daddy and Grandpa would go to the pig pond with their fishing poles. They'd bring back the most giant catfish you ever saw. Daddy said it was because they fed the fish so well. Plus, the water was deep. It was a flooded breather shaft for an old coal mine. Daddy said it was a hundred feet deep, with no shoreline. It just went straight down."

"So anyway, I was quiet for a minute, then I scratched my head and said, 'Daddy, you're talking about the pig pond, right?'"

"Daddy nodded. 'Yep. Your grandpa's dead, boy, so you and I are going to throw out all that hog shit.'"

"I was so excited that I could have jumped off the porch. But I knew better than to act so damn happy after all that happened, so I sat there with Daddy until he finished his coffee. Then, together, we went downstairs to the cellar."

"I always thought it was spooky down there when I was little. I never went down alone, that's for goddamn sure. Of course, if curiosity ever got the best of me, I would go down to the second step and look around, but that's as far as I would go."

"The floor was just your ordinary cement, and the walls were brick, nothing fancy. There were two doors, one outside that led into the cellar; that's how Daddy got them hogs down there, and another open doorway led into the living room. In one corner of the cellar, Daddy and Grandpa had built a holding pen for the hogs in one corner of the cellar. They did a great job on her, too. Daddy could weld some, so he got hold of some scrap rebar and did her up. It looked like a little jail cell like you see in the old

Westerns. Then, Daddy welded a small metal hoop inside the top of the pen. He said that way, he could wrap a chain around the hog's front legs and hang 'em if they were acting feisty."

"Next to the pen, there was one of the old-style bathtubs. That's where Daddy said he cut the hogs' throats. He said he would hold their heads inside the tub, pull their head back, and cut them. Daddy said they'd stop thrashing around if he did it quickly enough. Once they stopped moving, he would turn the water on, plop the hog inside, and gut them. When that was done, Daddy said he and Grandpa would take the guts and head and put them into trash bags. That way, they didn't drip all over and make a mess."

"They cut the meat in the tub. Daddy told me he usually did that. Daddy said Grandpa was too old to cut through the gristle and stuff. So his job was to wrap the meat in plastic sacks and put them in one of the deep freezers."

Zackary tapped his fingers restlessly against the arm of his wheelchair, rattling his restraints. Finally, he cleared his throat and continued.

"Well, there we were. Daddy had already bagged up the mess. They were sitting next to the tub. I remember the smell being awful. The insides of an animal are chock-full of shit and other nasty things."

"I asked Daddy, 'Daddy, before we go, can I see Grandpa?'"

"Daddy looked at me. 'Whatcha wanna do that for, boy?'"

"No reason, I guess. I just wanna see him, is all.'"

"Daddy shrugged. 'All right then.' Daddy walked over to the freezer closest to the stairs that led up into the living room. He looked back at me and said, 'Come on, boy, have a look.'"

"When Daddy opened the lid, I saw he had taken all the food out and spread it between the other two. That way, Grandpa would fit inside. I looked inside, and there he was. Grandpa still had Momma's towel wrapped around his neck. Momma or Daddy had crossed his hands over his chest, so he looked like he was sleeping. I was glad to see him looking so peaceful, especially after how he looked the night before. Other than the frost-forming patches on his hands and face, you wouldn't know Grandpa wasn't just sleeping. When Daddy figured I had seen enough, he closed the door."

"We both picked up two black trash bags each. Boy, I remember them being some heavy-ass bags, too. I'm telling you, Doctor, it sure seems like a lot gets wasted after you gut a hog."

From The Depths It Came

"Our walk was quiet. The trail was slippery that day because we had a lot of rain that night. I fell a few times, but I never asked Daddy to help me. See, I knew I was a man."

"It didn't take long to get to the pond. It was only a hundred feet through the woods. When we got there, the fog was still hovering over the water and surrounding reeds. It does that a lot. It's a low spot or something."

"Anyway, Daddy tossed the first bag into the water underhand style. You can't throw overhand because the pond is about twenty feet across. So after Daddy tossed his first bag in, I threw mine. When we were finished, he looked down at me. I could see he was proud by the look on his face."

"Boy, before we leave, we need to walk around the pond and make sure nothing floats up. Sometimes, the shafts down there don't take things away.' "What are we looking for, Daddy?"

"Anything that shouldn't be floating around a pond. Things like clothes, trash bags, that kinda shit."

"Daddy, why would clothes be floating around the pond?' "Daddy got a little mad at me. He said, 'Goddamnit, boy, stop asking so many fucking questions and do what I tell you.' "Okay, Daddy.' I was glad he hadn't slapped me like I was expecting."

"We started walking around the pond, and we ended up finding a few things—a couple of pieces of plastic bags caught up in the reeds and one old shirt tangled up in a branch over the water. Daddy and I tried to unwrap that damn shirt using sticks, but after a while, Daddy said, 'We ain't going to get it, boy. You've got to climb out there and grab it."

"I was scared to death; I didn't want to crawl out over that water." ' What if I fall in, Daddy? I can hardly swim."

"Daddy grabbed my shoulder hard and put his face close to mine.' Are you a man or some kinda little sissy bitch?"

"I tried not to cry and said, 'I'm a man, Daddy. Just a little scared."

"Scared or not, you've got to get out there and get that shirt. If I climb out there, the branch will snap. I'm too big. So you're going."

"I knew I had to prove I was a man, so I climbed slowly over the water, trying not to look down. When I got to the shirt, I started trying to pull it loose from the branch, but it was wrapped up pretty good. So I started tugging and pulling at it. That's when the branch snapped."

In the gloomy abyss, it stirred, sending tendrils of silt twirling around its dormant figure. Its eyes flickered open, drawn by a shadow crossing the surface above. It recognized the silhouette in the dim, turbid water –a child, but not any child, her child. Long had she languished, decomposing in the abyss, trapped within a catatonic prison of memories past. She had sensed his existence, glimpsed his vitality, and now, he was within her grasp.

Ascending from her muddied grave, she emerged from the depths with the stealth of a predator, yearning to claim him, to enfold herself in his living warmth once more.

"Now, Dr. Creed, I'm not sure how to explain this, but when I went under that water, I opened my eyes and looked down at my feet. There was a cloud of mud from somewhere far below, rising and swirling like smoke. It scared me. The first thing I thought was maybe I stirred up a giant-ass catfish or something. But it wasn't a catfish. Instead, two hands reached up out of that cloud of mud, then a face, a woman's awful rotting face. I'll never forget it. She had long blond hair still attached to that gray head of hers and the blackest eyes I had ever seen, and those eyes were looking right at me. When she got close enough, she tried grabbing my ankles, but I started kicking like hell. That didn't stop her, though."

"I looked up and saw that I was just inches from the surface, and Daddy was reaching out to me, so I stretched. Just as his fingers touched mine, she grabbed me and started making these awful sounds, like gurgling laughter. Thank God Daddy was stronger than she was. He yanked me out so hard that the next thing I knew, I was on my feet in front of him, dripping wet and crying like a baby."

"Daddy grabbed hold of me and hugged me real tight. Not so much because he gave a shit about me, but because he knew that if I had drowned, Momma would have been pissed, at least for a few hours until she got over it."

"I was so cold and shaking so hard that I thought I would freeze to death. I looked at Daddy and said, 'Daddy, I saw something. There was something in the water.' "Daddy looked me in the eye, then he looked over my shoulder at the pond and asked, 'What did you see in the water, boy?"

"My teeth were clacking together so hard I had a hell of a time telling him, but I said, 'Daddy, I saw a lady down there. I saw her come straight up from the bottom, and then she grabbed hold of me like she wanted to pull me back down with her."

"Daddy shook his head. 'Boy, let me tell you something. You didn't see any goddamn lady down there. You may have seen an old hog head floating around, but you didn't see a goddamn lady. And as far as something grabbing hold of you, it was that tree branch wrapped up in your clothes."

"I may have been a little kid, but I knew what I saw. 'Daddy, it was laughing or something."

"Daddy shook his head. 'No, boy, you heard me yelling for you to grab my hand. Have you ever held your head underwater and listened to someone outside it talking? It sounds funny. It doesn't sound like it does outside of water. That's on account of your ears getting all filled up. Now drop it. I'm taking you home. Don't tell Momma anything about what you thought you saw. She gets a little funny about that kind of stuff."

"Okay, Daddy, but what do I say about being all wet?"

"Well, there ain't nothing we can do about that. We'll just tell Momma you fell in. It was an accident, that's all."

"Is she gonna strap me, Daddy?"

"Daddy shrugged. 'Oh, probably, but I guess we won't know for sure until we get back to the house."

"I would have accepted this normally, but I was getting fed up. 'Daddy, you told me to go out there. It wasn't my fault."

"He slapped me on the side of my head pretty hard for saying that."

"Don't point fingers. Nobody cares about a snitch. Now, you'll take whatever you've got coming, understand?"

"I didn't think it was right, but I said, 'Okay, Daddy."

"Daddy fished that damn shirt out of the pond before we left. He looked around for a bit before he found a good-sized rock. Then he tied that damn shirt around it and tossed it into the pond."

"Guess I got lucky because when we got home, I didn't get strapped, but damn, did Daddy get hollered at. It really pissed Momma off that Daddy let me get so close to the water."

"Later that night, I woke up. It had to be late because Momma and Daddy were quiet. It was still dark outside, and the frogs and crickets were going at it, but they seemed louder than ever. Usually, I liked that sound, but the racket was too much. So, I figured if I was going to get any more sleep, I'd have to get up and close the window."

"I didn't want to wake up Momma and Daddy, so I carefully sat up and climbed out of bed, making sure my damn mattress wouldn't creak. Right before I got to the window, everything outside went dead silent."

"A strange feeling washed over me, like something was very wrong out there. I peeked out the window. There was just enough moonlight to light things up a bit. I saw nothing unusual, just a bunch of weeds and Daddy's rusted old cars scattered around the yard. I figured I must have let my imagination get the best of me."

"As I reached up to close the window, I noticed something. Someone was standing on the path leading to the pond, and they weren't moving. I didn't want the person to see me, so I stepped back from the window. That's when the lady I saw in the pond stepped out from under the shadows of the trees."

"She stood perfectly still with not a stitch of clothes on, and even though she was a fair distance away, I knew she was staring right at me. I didn't give a damn whether my bed creaked. I dove under my blankets and hid."

"I figured it wasn't long before she went back to the pond because the frogs and crickets started up again. That was good because I wasn't going to get up and close the window again."

"The next day, I woke up to Momma yelling from downstairs."

"Zack, get your ass down here and eat some breakfast." Of course, Daddy had to say something, too."

"You heard your momma. Get down here, you shit hog."

"I think sometimes he enjoyed making up names like that. It seemed he couldn't go through one day without calling me something. Momma wasn't much better."

"They were already sitting at the breakfast table when I entered the kitchen. Daddy glanced at me over his newspaper but said nothing. That was fine by me. I wasn't in the mood to hear his mouth anyway. Momma smiled at me before taking a sip of her coffee."

"Well, it's about time you climbed out of bed. I was just thinking you were going to sleep the whole day away."

"I didn't say anything, but the sun hadn't even come up yet, so I didn't know what she meant by sleeping the whole day away. I decided it would be best just to apologize."

"I'm sorry, Momma, I just couldn't sleep well."

"Momma smiled as she pointed to my plate. 'I made you a big plate of those pork chops you like, and I expect you to eat all of them. I fried up a whole mess of them. They were just starting to smell a little funny, and I won't have good meat going bad around here."

"Momma was right. I loved her pork chops, though I could have gone without hearing the meat smelled funny."

"When we were getting close to finishing up eating, Momma asked me, 'Is something on your mind, boy? You haven't said a word this whole time."

"Daddy set his napkin on the table, glaring at me. I think he was afraid I would mention something about the woman in the pond."

"Well, Momma, there is something.' I glanced at Daddy. 'Did you hear the frogs last night?"

"Momma laughed. 'Well, what the hell kind of question is that? We hear them every night."

"Well, did you hear them get loud and then stop?"

"Momma thought for a second," 'I can't say I did." Momma looked at Daddy. 'Did you hear anything like that, Daddy?"

"Nope, sounds like you must have had a bad dream or something."

"It wasn't a bad dream, Daddy. The crickets and frogs got really loud, and when I got up to close my window, I saw a lady standing on the trail near the pond."

"Momma looked scared. 'Why didn't you wake us up? We can't have people sneaking around here. No telling what someone might do way the hell up here."

"Daddy pounded his fist on the table so hard the dishes rattled. 'Goddamnit, boy, if you ever see someone sneaking around here, we got to know about it!"

"Well, Daddy, I was afraid to wake you up. I thought I might have got beat if I did."

"Daddy was turning red in the face. It looked like he was fixing to beat me right then and there, but Momma interrupted him before he could."

"What did she look like?" she asked, standing up.

"I knew I would get a beating regardless of what I told them, so I went ahead and just said it. 'It was a naked, rotting lady with long blond hair, and she was looking right up at me."

"Momma sat back down and looked at Daddy."

"You say she had long blond hair?"

"She sure did, long blond hair, and she was naked."

"Momma looked at Daddy. They didn't seem concerned about the naked part, but I could tell the blond-haired lady meant something."

"Daddy,' Momma said, 'there hasn't been a single woman up this way with blond hair except for you know who. The rest of them had brown hair."

"I know, Momma. I think I know what this is all about."

"They both looked at me, just staring for a while. I wasn't sure what they were thinking, but it made me fidget in my chair. It was Daddy who broke the silence."

"Boy, there is something you should know, and I don't think you'll like it."

"He was right. I did not like what he had to say one bit."

Secrets Revealed

"Daddy took Momma's hand in his. Then, just as he said, he laid it all out."

"We aren't your parents by blood. Why do you think your hair is blond and ours is black? That's because you had a different momma and daddy before we took you in as our own."

"I felt like someone had punched me in the stomach. How could I have a different momma and daddy? I would've thought he was playing a dirty joke on me, but I could tell by his face that he wasn't."

"Your grandpa came across your real momma and daddy when you were about two. They were camped in the woods about a half-mile or so from here. Your grandpa happened to be out and about when he saw their campfire. He said he walked up on them and told them that he got himself turned around and was lost."

"Your grandpa said they were really nice German people, but they didn't speak much English. During their talk, they told your grandpa that they were on a cross-country camping tour. Your grandpa pretended to be interested, got them to trust him, and asked if he could bed down by their fire until dawn. They agreed."

"Your grandpa said they were talking late before he got tired of their company. So he stood up like he was going to take a piss. That was when he attacked them with his hunting knife. He said your Daddy was the first to go. Grandpa got him right across the throat. Your momma was a different story. She tried running inside their tent. I guess she put up a hell of a fight. Grandpa said he lost count of how many times he had to stab her, but eventually, he got the job done."

"That's when he heard crying coming from inside the tent. When he opened it, two little twin boys were sitting on a sleeping bag, crying and carrying on for their momma. One of those boys was you. Your grandpa wasn't sure what to do. He wanted a grandson, and he knew your momma, and I couldn't have any, so he took one. He chose you and left the other one behind."

"When he got home, he woke your momma and me up and gave you to us to raise as our own. So we did. I always knew you wouldn't amount to shit, and your momma and grandpa soon found out I was right."

"I felt so sick to my stomach. I thought I would throw up all over that damn kitchen table. I probably should have been frightened, but my anger finally won out. I tried to keep my voice as even as possible."

"So what happened to my brother? Did you leave him out there to die?"

"Daddy cleared his throat. 'Well, no. Me and your grandpa went back to the campsite the next morning. We dug a deep hole and laid your daddy down in it. Neither of us had the heart to kill a baby, so we put him in the grave with your daddy and buried him up so we didn't have to hear him crying. Then we cleaned up the campsite and drove the car they rented back here."

"What about my momma? What did you do with her?"

"Well, we took her body to the pond and sank her. Now that's the entire story, and that's that."

"At that moment, I wanted to kill my momma and daddy. I decided to do just that once I was older and stronger.

"It's not just 'that's that,' Daddy. Tell him about the house," said Momma.

"Dammit, Momma, I got things I want to get done today. I'm sick of telling all these damn stories."

"I said to tell him. Now do it."

"Daddy knew better than to argue with Momma, so on he went."

"Boy, it's like this. This whole place is chock-full of ghosts, and it would be a lie for me to sit here and tell you that your momma or I haven't seen or heard them. Some mind their business, some don't. Sometimes, they just wander around a bit. Other times, they get a little mischievous and mess with your mind. The bottom line is this is one damn haunted house. There's been more killing done on this land and in this house than probably anywhere for a hundred miles around. So I guess I'm saying the blond woman you saw was your momma's spirit. I don't know why she's started coming around now, but she has, and we're just going to live with it."

"My head was swimming. I had to leave that house and get away from Momma and Daddy for a while. I turned to Momma. 'If it's okay, I want to go outside and be alone for a while."

"I didn't expect her to say yes, but she showed an unnerving amount of sympathy given what I now knew.."

"You run along, boy. I'll take care of clearing the table."

"I sat on the front porch and stared down the path leading to the pond. Part of me thought I would be better off if I jumped in and let my real momma take me to the bottom with her. Maybe that was what she wanted. Maybe she wanted me to be with her. But why now, after all these years had gone by?"

"As I sat there thinking about everything Daddy had told me, I noticed the birds had stopped singing. There was an eerie silence, just like the night before. From inside the house, I heard Momma clanking dishes and Daddy talking to her about something stupid, but the woods outside were still."

"I looked toward the pond just as a flock of birds flew from the trees in all directions. Something had sent them into a panic, and I saw why the lady, my real momma, was walking up the trail from the pond. She stopped when she reached the edge of the trees, just like she had done the night before."

"For some reason, I wasn't afraid of her anymore. Though I thought it was strange that a ghost would be out during daylight. That was my first lesson in dealing with the dead. They show up whenever they want to, day or night."

"I glanced behind me to make sure Momma and Daddy weren't watching and then started walking toward her. She never took her eyes off me, and I did the same to her."

"When I got within ten feet of her, I stopped. We both just stood there, neither one of us moving an inch. It was so quiet I could hear the drops of water tapping on the ground from her dripping hair."

"I tried to imagine what her gray face must have looked like when she was alive, but she had been dead for quite a while. The mud on her face didn't help matters either. You wouldn't have known if she had been a pretty woman. Time had not been kind."

"She had open black gashes on her chest and stomach. I figured they must have got there when Grandpa stabbed her to death. She must have known what I was thinking. She looked down at her chest before raising her arm slowly and pointing toward the house. I had a feeling she was trying to tell me something, so I asked the first thing that came to mind."

"Are you looking for my grandpa because of what he did to you?"

She turned slowly as if to say no but pointed toward the house.

"Are you looking for my daddy?"

She nodded her head in agreement.

"Are you looking for my daddy because of what he did to my brother?"

Again, she nodded, but her finger still pointed towards the house. It suddenly struck me that Daddy had always been a liar, so why would this be any different?

"Are you trying to tell me Daddy is the one who killed you?"

She lowered her arm and returned toward the pond, whispering, "Yes."

It didn't come as a surprise to me. Daddy was the one responsible for killing my family. What angered me more was that he had lied about it and blamed Grandpa, even though I knew Grandpa was capable of the same deeds if given the chance".

"I followed her back to the pond, hoping to find answers to my questions, but she remained silent, refusing to speak."

"When we reached the shore, something came over me, and I said, "I love you, Momma.""

"I don't know why I said that. I guess I still had feelings for her from when I was little, and even though she was dead, I think she still loved me. That bothered me; if Daddy hadn't killed her, I believe she would have loved and cared for me as a mother should."

"She looked back and pointed at me as if returning my affection. Then, without another word, she stepped into the pond and disappeared, leaving behind a small circle of rippled water. But that wasn't the last time I saw her."

The Ballad of the Hunter and the Prey

"Life carried on as usual for a few months after that incident. Then, one night after supper, I noticed Daddy unusually dressed up. I was sitting at the kitchen table, coloring on some old newspapers he had given me."

"Momma looked up from her dishes, clearly taken aback by Daddy's appearance. He wore his only nice T-shirt, as the rest were full of moth holes. He also had on his only good pair of pants."

"Momma said, 'You sexy man, why don't you ever get all spiffed up for me?'"

"Daddy chuckled and walked over to her, giving her a gentle squeeze on her behind. 'Just wait till I get home, baby doll,' he said, clearly in good spirits."

"Curiosity getting the better of me, I asked, Daddy, where are you going?'"

"I knew he didn't have a regular job, though he occasionally did odd jobs around town. But tonight, he seemed different."

"I've got some adult things to take care of tonight, so don't worry about it. You understand, boy?' he replied."

"Having learned the truth about him, his threats didn't scare me as much anymore. I knew he could have killed me if he wanted to, but he hadn't."

"Okay, Daddy, I understand,' "I said, trying to act like I wasn't interested anyway."

"Daddy kissed Momma and patted my head before heading to the front door. He turned to us before leaving, saying, 'Momma, I'm gonna be late, so don't wait up."

"Momma blew him a kiss and playfully replied, 'You always say that, and I always wait up."

"Daddy left, and I heard the old truck roaring to life outside. He was off to wherever he had to go, so I went on with my coloring while Momma finished up the dishes. She eventually sat beside me and said, 'Boy, why don't you come to the cellar with me? I want to pray for your grandpa."

"Daddy still hadn't buried Grandpa, and we sometimes visited him in the cellar, talking to him as if he were still alive."

"Together, we went down to the cellar, Momma holding my hand. She turned on two lights, and we stood over Grandpa, his body now covered in frost. Momma looked down at me, a serious expression on her face."

"There's something I need to tell you, but you have to promise not to tell your daddy,' she said."

"I promise, Momma,' I replied, eager to know what she had to say. "I won't say anything, Momma."

"Well, your daddy is going to the city tonight. It's a couple of hours from here, so as he said, he won't be home until almost morning. He might ask you to help him down here when he gets back. He told me the other night that he thinks you're old enough to learn how to kill one of those hogs. You're the same age he was when Grandpa and Grandma taught him how, so he figured tonight's the night. It's going to be important you listen to your daddy when he's talking to you. He's going to show you how to do some things you'll have to know, especially once your daddy and I get too old and can't. So you be brave and do what he asks you, okay?"

"I was a little scared, but I'd be lying if I said I wasn't excited at the same time."

"Okay, Momma."

"Momma hugged me and said, 'Well then, let's pray daddy makes it home safe and that he brings us home a big surprise."

Charlie was on the prowl, a relentless predator with senses honed to a savage edge. His eyes roamed the darkened streets of St. Louis, akin to a prowling lion surveilling the African grasslands for its next kill. With a measured pace, he cruised through the city's shadowed alleys, surveying clusters of vulnerable souls - prostitutes and the homeless, seeking the faintest hint of fragility.

Charlie turned left off Boulder Avenue onto Riverview, savoring the familiar gloom that blanketed the street. Here, he found his comfort zone, a place inhabited exclusively by society's cast-offs - individuals who could vanish without a trace, their absence unnoticed and unremarkable.

By midnight, the neighborhood's inhabitants emerged from their squalid, rat-infested dwellings to roam the desolate streets. Charlie's eyes briefly caught the furtive movements of these individuals, lurking in the darkness like cockroaches, wary of venturing into the light.

Some were cautious, biding their time until it was safe to come out. However, in this unforgiving urban wilderness, there was always one emboldened by false confidence or complacency who would become easy prey for whatever dangers lurked in the shadows.

It didn't take long before Charlie spotted his victim. He couldn't help but smile. She was strolling alone in the same direction he was driving.

Charlie slowly drove past her, sizing up his victim. She had shoulder-length brown hair and wore a red skirt far too short and a tight red skirt. Her top appeared nothing more than a bikini, and on her feet were a pair of scuffed and battered black spiked pumps.

Charlie brought his truck to a halt by the curb, waiting patiently. His eyes fixed on her through the rear-view mirror as she drew near. It was clear to him that she'd make for an easy target.

Nineteen-year-old Linda Stewart couldn't help but sigh under her breath as she made her way home. It had been a slow night at work, but that was par for the course on a Monday. On top of that, she'd been battling a nasty cold for over a week, and all she wanted was to collapse onto her bed and drift into a peaceful slumber. But as fate would have it, this night held something entirely different for her.

As Linda approached the truck's passenger side, she momentarily considered walking past but reminded herself that it would be over in ten minutes, and judging by the truck's appearance, she doubted he'd have enough money for a hand job.

As she reached the passenger door, Linda mumbled, "Remember to smile."

As she approached the truck's cab, Linda squinted in the dimly lit street. The driver remained a mysterious figure, hidden in the shadows. She hesitated briefly before giving the window a gentle tap.

Out of the darkness, a pale hand extended towards the door, unlocking it. Linda glanced up and down the street, ensuring it was safe, before gingerly opening the door.

Inside the truck's shadowy interior, a grotesque man came into view. His appearance was far from pleasant, but Linda fought back her repulsion, forcing a smile. "Can I help you with something?"

Charlie's grin widened. This was going to be easier than he thought. She looked young and fragile, unlikely to pose any threat. Playing the nice guy was a role he could perform with ease.

"Sweetheart," he began, feigning charm, "I was just wondering if you're available for some work tonight?"

Linda turned on her flirtatious charm, meeting his gaze. "Could be," she purred. "What are you looking for, honey?"

Charlie had played this cat-and-mouse game countless times. It no longer held his interest, but he kept up the act.

"I was thinking we could go all the way," he replied with a sly grin.

Linda smirked back at him, her tone dripping with suggestion. "It won't come cheap, you know."

Charlie chuckled, a wicked glint in his eyes. "Well, good thing I'm not looking for a bargain."

As the conversation continued, Linda couldn't ignore the putrid stench of his breath. She braced herself for the disgusting encounter.

"How much you got on you, mister?" she asked.

Charlie laughed. "Now, girl, this ain't the first time I've done this. I ain't gonna tell you how much I got, or you'll want it all. Now quit playing games and tell me how much you are going to fucking cost me?"

Linda laughed, realizing he'd seen through her little act. "For the whole shebang, it's a hundred bucks."

Charlie nodded, feigning contemplation. "A little steep, ain't it, girl?"

Linda remained firm. "Well, if you want it all, that's what it's gonna cost you."

After a moment of pretend consideration, Charlie gestured toward the truck. "Well, hop in." He patted the seat invitingly.

Linda grinned but didn't close the door behind her. Instead, she extended her left hand. "Pay me first," she said firmly.

Charlie shook his head. "I ain't paying you beforehand. How do I know you won't run off the second that cash hits your hands?"

Linda hesitated for a moment, glancing at her apartment building across the street. She entertained the thought of calling off the encounter and retreating to the safety of her home. However, the pressing need for money forced her hand.

She turned her attention back to Charlie. "Alright," she said, "show me you've got the money."

Charlie shook his head slightly, his frustration evident. He reached into his back pocket and retrieved his wallet.

"Goddamn, girl, you sure are making this a real pain in the ass." He opened his tattered wallet, pulling out a wrinkled hundred-dollar bill. He waved it at Linda. "There it is, darlin'. Are you happy now?"

Linda wasn't happy, but she shut the door and pointed toward the end of the street. "Go that way. There's a place I like to use."

Charlie rubbed his hands together, a wicked grin creeping across his face. "Well, all right then."

He drove to the end of the street, arriving at a cul-de-sac. The lone streetlight above it had long been shattered, casting a veil of darkness. Yet, it was a perfect spot for the local prostitutes to conduct their business. If the police happened to turn onto Riverview, the prostitutes could quickly escape from their client's vehicle, vanishing into the labyrinth of nearby apartment buildings.

Charlie parked his truck, facing the direction he had come from, and switched off his headlights. The darkness concealed his sinister intentions.

Linda peered at him, silently thanking the cover of darkness that spared her from seeing his face.

"You got a rubber?" she inquired.

"Yeah," Charlie responded, his voice a mix of eagerness and something more sinister. "It's in the glove compartment."

He leaned over, his movements unsettlingly close, and reached across her lap. The greasy strands of hair that clung to the back of his head brushed against her mouth. Linda recoiled, repulsed by his unwashed stench, as if he hadn't bathed in weeks.

Charlie rummaged through the glove compartment, pretending to search for the condom.

"I know it's here. So damn dark I can't see," he grumbled.

Linda couldn't stand his greasy hair brushing against her face any longer, so she turned her head toward the passenger door.

"It's okay. I've got one."

Charlie let out a low, gruff laugh. "Well, shit, girl, you should've said that."

Charlie's heart raced, adrenaline coursing through his veins as the moment of attack approached. Suddenly, he sat up, launching his brutal assault. His elbow struck her forehead with a sickening thud, sending her head hurtling backward into the rear window, cracking it from top to bottom.

Linda collapsed forward, unconscious. Charlie grabbed the back of her head, pushing her face into her lap. He quickly searched his surroundings. He saw no one and nothing other than his cracked rear window.

Rage surged within him like a spark igniting gasoline. No one had ever damaged his truck, and the fury burned fiercely. Blinded by an internal rage, Charlie savagely pounded the back of Linda's head until he noticed blood on his hands. He wasn't sure if it had come from his knuckles or Linda's head.

"You stupid fucking whore. Look what you did, goddamn it."

Charlie fought the urge to snap her neck. As much as he wanted to, he couldn't do that, not yet. He had to get her home and do it right.

Charlie reached under his seat, snatching a roll of duct tape and quickly wrapping her hands and feet before covering her eyes and mouth. When he finished, he shoved the tape back under his seat and pushed Linda's unconscious body onto the floorboard. Charlie took a deep breath before eyeing the surrounding area.

Still, everything seemed normal. Charlie turned the key in the ignition, and his old truck, reliable as ever, roared to life. He flicked on the headlights and drove calmly toward Boulder Avenue. He came to a complete stop at the stop sign, checking for any oncoming traffic. The streets were deserted, with no vehicles in sight. He eased onto Boulder Avenue, heading east toward Highway 30.

Half a block away, facing the opposite direction, Officer Gary Hinkle was parked in his police cruiser. Through a pair of department-issued night vision binoculars, Hinkle read the license plate on the old Chevy pulling out of Riverview Drive. It was the eighteenth vehicle he had observed leaving the drug-infested area during the last four hours. He reached for his radio.

"Thirty-two, Paul, one."

The dispatcher's monotone voice answered,

"Thirty-two-one."

"Are you clear to check a plate?"

Dispatch responded in the same uninterested tone.

"Sorry, thirty-two-one, the system is down."

"Ten-four," Hinkle sighed as he acknowledged the transmission. He had diligently run the license plates of every vehicle exiting Riverview Drive. He anticipated that a parolee's vehicle would inevitably leave the neighborhood, and he was determined to be there when it did.

As he contemplated pursuing the truck, Hinkle knew he could likely find a reason to pull it over. He checked his rear-view mirror and saw no other vehicles approaching. With a sense of purpose, he left the curb and accelerated towards the distant taillights.

Charlie felt a sense of unease, but everything appeared to be going smoothly thus far. He was approaching the on-ramp, and from there, he would drive two miles before heading north. After that, he'd be in the clear, marking another successful hunt. He glanced down at Linda, whose head gently rocked with the motion of the truck. That's good, Charlie thought. There's nothing worse than having to pull off the side of the road with a wriggling, taped-up woman in the front seat of your car. He had been there and done that.

Charlie's heart raced as he glanced up at his rear-view mirror. The rapidly approaching headlights revealed a vehicle with a light bar on its roof, unmistakably a police cruiser. He knew he had to get off the road before the cruiser caught up with him. There was a Darby's burger shack about a block ahead. If he could make it there, he could pull in and pretend to be getting something to eat. He doubted the cop would follow him into the drive-through. Charlie sped up slightly, trying not to make it obvious to the approaching cruiser.

Officer Hinkle managed to catch up with the truck, narrowing the distance to within two car lengths. He scrutinized it, looking for any valid reason to pull it over. He mentally ticked off the items on his checklist: the registration was up to date, the taillights were operational, and the headlights were working correctly. No visible safety hazards were present. Despite the truck's unappealing appearance, he lacked a legal justification to stop it.

Hinkle continued to trail the truck, employing a classic police strategy. He was aware that seeing a police cruiser in a driver's rear-view mirror often induced anxiety and distraction. Drivers might become more preoccupied with the presence of the police officer behind them, potentially leading to errors like crossing the yellow line or neglecting to use their turn signals, ultimately providing grounds for a traffic stop.

A block later, the truck's right-turn signal flickered to life, and it pulled into the Darby's burger shack. Officer Hinkle knew the driver had noticed him, and the cat-and-mouse game had begun. He was confident the driver had something to hide. Those with guilty consciences often sought refuge in gas stations or store parking lots, feigning innocence in the hope that the police would move on. However, Hinkle had time on his side; his shift didn't end until 6:00 a.m.

Much to his dismay, Charlie cautiously entered Darby's drive-through as he hadn't planned to drive through a well-lit area with a bound woman on his floorboard. Yet, he felt he had no other option. If he turned back onto the street, he believed the cop would pull him over. So, he proceeded with care toward the menu sign.

Hinkle followed the truck into the parking lot, taking note of the crack in the rear window as the driver passed the brightly lit menu sign. "Got 'em," he muttered to himself. However, Hinkle decided to let the driver stew for a little while. He parked his cruiser nearby and patiently waited for the truck to complete its circuit around the building.

As the crackling male voice repeated his order, Charlie proceeded to window number one as instructed. Nervously, he stole a glance at the woman lying beside him. Attempting to conceal her, Charlie contorted sideways and was astonished at how easily he could hide her from view.

The teenage boy working at the drive-through appeared too engrossed in his cell phone conversation to pay much attention. Without making eye contact, he handed Charlie a grease-spotted bag of food and abruptly closed the window.

Driving away from the window, Charlie grumbled, "That little fuck didn't even give me my damn drink." He might have contemplated shooting the boy inside the restaurant in different circumstances, but he had far more pressing matters on his mind.

Charlie drove around the building, heading for the exit, and strained to spot the police cruiser, but it was nowhere in sight. He stopped, flipped on his right blinker, and merged onto Boulder Avenue. The on-ramp loomed less than a quarter-mile away. Darby's was the final business in the vicinity, and beyond it lay only vacant, heavily wooded lots. There would be no parking lots to slip into if the police cruiser got behind him.

Peering at his rear-view mirror, Charlie spotted the police cruiser with its flashing red and blue lights exiting Darby's parking lot and speeding in his direction. Adrenaline surged through his body, causing a fit of coughing.

Anticipating the inevitable, Charlie reached behind the backrest and fumbled for his .38.

Officer Hinkle's cruiser rumbled to a stop behind the suspicious truck, its red brake lights illuminating the darkness. With a flick of the switch, Hinkle bathed the scene in the harsh glare of his spotlight, casting long shadows across the road. The malfunctioning radio crackled intermittently, a reminder of the night's eerie atmosphere.

As Hinkle approached, his trained eye caught sight of the forged registration tags, a deceptive attempt to evade detection. He made a swift decision, opting to impound the truck and let towing and storage fees do their work, effectively removing another piece of shit from the streets.

With a sense of foreboding, Charlie rolled down his window, squinting against the blinding light of the spotlight. His heart raced as he watched Hinkle's approach, his nerves taut with anticipation.

In the tense silence, Hinkle closed in, his flashlight casting ominous shadows. Charlie's grip tightened around the gun in his lap, his pulse pounding in his ears. With a steady hand, he raised the weapon, his actions betraying his desperate resolve.

In a split second, the scene erupted into chaos. A gunshot shattered the silence, followed by the sickening thud of a bullet finding its mark. Officer Hinkle's lifeless body crumpled to the ground, the smile of his killer etched in his final moments of terror.

In the aftermath, only silence remained, broken only by the faint squawk of Officer Hinkle's radio.

Charlie stomped on the gas pedal, screeching the tires as he fled the scene for home. He looked in his rear-view mirror. The officer was lying spread-eagle on the pavement where he had collapsed, his dutiful cruiser behind him, still flashing its red and blues.

As far as Charlie could see, there wasn't another car on the road. He accelerated onto the Highway 30 on-ramp, all the while laughing uncontrollably. He had never killed a cop, and the excitement of the act threw him into unabashed euphoria. Charlie howled into the night before turning up the crackling stereo to a long-forgotten country and western song.

Three highway patrol units sped past him in the opposite direction a few minutes later. Someone had discovered the dead officer. He watched their flashing lights recede into the distance in his rear-view mirror. As the lights faded, he pressed down on the gas pedal. He knew he had to put as much distance as possible between himself and the place where he had killed the cop. His initial excitement had now morphed into fear. He had to get home quickly, knowing that the police would soon search for the person who had killed one of their own.

First Kill

"It must have been around three-thirty in the morning when I heard Grandpa's truck roaring up the driveway. I jumped up and looked out of my bedroom window. Daddy had kicked up so much dust that I could hardly see him. I had never seen him drive like that, and I knew something was wrong."

"The porch light turned on, and I guessed Momma was still waiting for him. Daddy got out of the truck and slammed his door shut behind him. I could see he was shaken up from the way he walked. He rushed to the truck's passenger side and opened the door. By then, Momma was outside, opening the cellar doors. What I saw next scared the life out of me."

"Daddy grabbed hold of two legs that were taped together and pulled them from Grandpa's truck. From where I was, it looked like a woman all taped up. Daddy wasn't gentle with her either. He yanked her out of the truck and let her fall hard onto the ground. Momma walked over to Daddy, saying something, so I slid the window open to hear what was happening.

"You heard me, Daddy. Did you touch her? Did you foul her?" "Momma asked with fear in her voice."

Daddy looked at Momma intensely and replied, "No, goddamn it, and don't worry about that. We've got bigger problems."

"What? What did you do?" "asked Momma, sounding terrified."

"I killed a cop, Momma. I had to shoot that son of a bitch right in the goddamn face. The motherfucker didn't give me any other choice."

"Momma looked down towards the road and then back at Daddy."

"They didn't come after you, did they?"

"No, they didn't come after me, but that doesn't mean they won't either."

"Well, what the hell are we going to do?" Momma asked.

"Right now, we've got to get this woman in the cellar. Then I'm going to get rid of the plates on that truck and put the real ones back on."

"Momma pointed at the license plate on the front bumper. 'Well, aren't those the license plates?"

"They ain't the ones that go to this truck. Those belong on that old Chevy we got around back, and that one ain't registered to me or anybody else around these parts. I got her from the McLain's down Pine Valley way a long time back. Now, Momma, help with this woman. Come on now."

"I watched them pick up that woman and start for the cellar doors. When I lost sight of them, I ran back to my bed and hid under the blankets. I hoped they wouldn't call me down there to help."

Linda's eyes fluttered open, but her vision was hazy, making it hard to comprehend her dire situation. It all felt like some surreal nightmare. What was clear was that she was being carried, and she recognized the stench of the man who had deceived her earlier. However, there was another presence, a woman's voice murmuring nearby. Linda strained to understand the words but couldn't quite make them out. Nevertheless, in her disoriented state, she held onto a glimmer of hope that this woman might show compassion.

With her remaining specks of strength, Linda fought against her captors, but it proved futile. Her attempts to gnaw through the tape and reach her captor's leg ended in despair. They found her struggles amusing, laughing at her feeble attempts, which only added to her torment.

"Momma, look at this crazy bitch trying to bite my leg. Have you ever seen something like that?" Charlie laughed.

"No, I can't say I have. You're lucky you taped her mouth up, or she would have latched onto you like a snapping turtle."

Charlie and Darleen laughed as they stumbled down the stairs into the shadowy depths of the cellar with their wriggling catch.

Upon reaching the cage, Charlie forcefully raised Linda's arms toward the ceiling and fastened her wrists to the chain hanging from above. Linda was left dangling, her body suspended above the floor, helpless and in agony. Charlie stepped back with a satisfied smirk, reveling in his cruel handiwork.

"I think that will do it, Momma. Let's get her clothes off so the boy won't have to do it in the morning."

Darleen grimaced, "I don't want him doing that. He's not old enough to be taking clothes off a grown woman."

Linda's mind snapped into focus, and the repulsive man's intentions became painfully clear. Fueled by terror, she intensified her struggle to break free. Her frantic writhing against the restraints only resulted in Darleen's powerful arms locking around her knees like a vice, rendering her immobile.

Charlie ripped Linda's clothes from her before exiting the cage again with Darleen at his side. He put his arm around Darleen's shoulder.

"Well, Momma, we may be older, but we still got it."

Darleen glanced up at Charlie, then at the naked woman hanging in the cage. She was still squirming to free herself.

"Daddy, are you sure you got her tied up good? I don't want it getting loose and running around the house."

"Of course, I got her tied up. She's not going anywhere."

Darleen yawned. "Well, if that's the case, I'm going to bed. I've had about all the bullshit I can handle for one night."

Charlie sealed the cage door with a rusty padlock, testing its security with a tug to ensure there was no escape. He stashed the key safely in the top drawer of his toolbox. Charlie left only one bulb shining above the pen, dimming the lights in the basement. With his arm draped over Darleen's shoulders, he led her up the stairs, leaving behind the horrific scene below.

Linda was naked, cold, and painfully hanging in a cage. She knew there was no chance of escape. Wherever she was would be where she died. Linda always knew she would die a violent death. That was just how it went when you lived and worked among the dregs of society. But this—what the fuck kind of bullshit was this? No heroic last stand in the streets, no grand final battle against an evil assailant. Nothing. A quick blow to the face, followed by darkness. Linda was angry. She would rather they had just got it over with.

"I woke up to Daddy sitting on my bed, with Momma standing behind him. Both were smiling at me. I didn't know why they were smiling, but I knew I wouldn't like it."

"Well, boy, today's the day. Today, you're going to help me do something really special,' Daddy said while rubbing my head."

"I looked at Momma. She was tearing up some."

"That's right, baby doll. Today, you'll learn how to do a man's job."

"Daddy, I don't want to help anyone if it's about that lady you got holed up in the cellar."

"Daddy glanced back at Momma. I knew I'd pissed him off."

"Now listen. You never tell me you ain't going to help me with something. You ain't old enough to be talking that kind of shit to me in my house, and how do you know what we got in the cellar? Have you been spying like a little piece of shit? Were you hiding around the house, maybe lying outside me and your momma's bedroom door, sticking your ears to the floor, listening and shit?"

"I didn't know what the hell he was talking about. I looked over his shoulder at Momma. She just stood there, not saying a goddamn thing in my defense. She seemed pretty pissed off too. I wasn't sure what to say, so I just said, 'No, Daddy, I haven't been sneaking around."

"That was when he did it. He backhanded me square in the mouth so hard I smacked my head off the headboard—split my lip all to shit. I started bleeding pretty badly. I just started crying and trying not to let blood get on my bed or pajamas. I looked up, holding on to my mouth with both hands and here came Momma like a lion. She pushed Daddy out of her way and punched me right in my stomach. She knocked all the wind right out of me. I curled up in a ball, and she just started in, beating me all up and down. It seemed like it went on for a long time before she finally stopped."

"She fell beside me, all out of breath, and cried like she was the one who got kicked to shit. I wasn't sure what to think. Then, as if nothing had just happened, she put her arms around me and said, 'I love you, boy. I love you so much, but don't you ever sneak around again."

"Now I don't know. Maybe Momma didn't hear me when I said I hadn't been sneaking around, but I wasn't about to argue, so I just balled up in her arms. 'Okay, Momma, I won't be sneaking around anymore, I promise."

"I know you won't, baby doll. I know you won't ever be bad again."

"After a few minutes, she sat up with me and reached out to Daddy. We kind of had a little family hug before Daddy said, 'As soon as you finish breakfast, you're gonna be helping me in the cellar."

"Okay, Daddy."

"He smiled at me and took me out of Momma's arms. Then he carried me downstairs to the kitchen table and cleaned me up with an old wet towel. Not one of Momma's good ones, though. Then we ate breakfast together as a family should. Although my lips burned really bad, I acted like the beating had never happened. I wish I could say that was the end of the beatings, but they became much worse as the years went on."

"Once we finished breakfast, Momma started clearing the table."

"It's time we get busy, boy. Let's go," said Daddy. "He led me down the stairs and into the cellar. The only light on was the one nearest to the pigpen. Daddy didn't like to waste electricity. So, with only one light, it was hard to see into the pen. But I knew that lady was in there. I could see her. She was hanging by her wrists from that chain Daddy had rigged up."

"As I walked closer to the pen, I saw it. It looked like a pink hog all strung up until Daddy turned on the other lights. I could see it wasn't a hog. It was a lady, and she wasn't wearing any clothes. I looked up at

Daddy. He was just standing there, grinning. He looked like he was proud of what he'd done."

"I looked back at the lady and noticed she wasn't moving, so I asked Daddy, 'Is she dead?"

"Daddy patted my head. 'No, she's just pretending. They do that sometimes, thinking you might leave them alone and not finish the job."

"I was a little confused, so I asked Daddy, 'So why do we have this lady strung up in the pigpen?"

"Daddy looked down at me, smiling, and said, 'Boy, that ain't no lady. It's a hog. It's one of the magic ones. They are good at playing tricks on a boy's mind. You know, like making a boy think it's a lady when it isn't."

"Daddy, why would it want to play magic tricks on me?"

"I told you it doesn't want you to kill it, boy."

"I was getting uncomfortable with the whole situation, so I spoke my mind. 'Well, I don't want to kill it, Daddy. It doesn't look like a hog. It looks like a naked lady."

"Daddy smacked me hard in the back of my head. 'I told you it ain't no fucking lady, and if you keep arguing with me, I'll kick the holy shit right outta you and string you up in there with it."

"I stood there for a minute, rubbing my head. I didn't know what the fuck was going on. That was not a hog hanging in that old pen. I decided to go along with whatever I was told. So I said, Okay, Daddy."

"Daddy smiled. 'Okay then, first off, you're going to start acting like a man and not some back-talking little shit. No one likes a back-talking little shit. Parents expect their kids to do what they say with no sass. That shows a kid's parents that they respect what they say."

"Yes, Daddy."

"That made Daddy happy. He squeezed my shoulder, then walked to the tub. He took his special toolbox off the shelf above. I knew he kept his butchering tools in it, and I knew those butchering tools were special to him. So when he handed me the toolbox, I didn't know what to think."

"Now listen to me, boy. These tools don't just belong to me anymore. They belong to you too. You'll have to help me take good care of them; they were your grandpa's, and some were even his grandpa's. A man's tools should mean as much to him as his wife and kids. That means keeping them in a safe place, clean and sharp."

Daddy patted my head, smiling, "Now line them up next to the tub. We've got work to do."

"Daddy took two rubber aprons down off the wall. He handed me one and said, 'This was your grandpa's apron. He would have wanted you to have it. It's a family tradition around here. Once a man in our family gets too old to do his job or dies, he hands down his things to his son or grandson. That way, the family keeps living like they always have. It's how we survive. Now put it on, boy."

"I put on Grandaddy's apron. It was way too big for me and sagging to the floor."

"Once I got it on, Daddy said, 'Put the toolbox down on the table next to the tub."

"I did what he said but wasn't sure what to do next, so I just stood there, waiting for Daddy to tell me what to do."

"Daddy smiled before whispering, 'Now you listen to me, boy. You do everything I tell you. You can't fuck this up. If this hog gets loose, it could rip your throat out like what happened to your grandpa. So we have to work fast. Do you understand me?"

"Even though I was terrified, I knew Daddy knew what he was doing, and I sure as hell didn't want my throat ripped all to shit, so I said, 'I understand, Daddy. I'll do whatever you tell me."

"Good; now open the top drawer on the toolbox and get me the keys."

"I handed the keys to Daddy. He took them, then walked to the door of the pen. I held my breath while he unlocked the door. He opened it real slow, then looked back at me and put his fingers to his lips like he wanted me to be quiet. Then he pointed to the toolbox."

"I looked into it, then at him. I wasn't sure what he wanted me to do. He started making hand motions for me to take something out of the box. So I grabbed the first thing I saw. It was a knife. A big one, and by the look of it, it was a real old one too. But goddamn, that thing was sharp, as if it was brand-new."

"I looked over at Daddy. He smiled and nodded. Then he unlocked the chain wrapped around that woman's wrist. That was when I noticed she had started shaking."

"Daddy was right. She wasn't dead after all. As soon as she knew her hands were free, she started hollering and thrashing around, but she couldn't make much noise because her mouth was taped up. She couldn't move much either. She just wiggled in Daddy's arms like a big worm as he dragged her across the floor."

"Daddy forced her to the ground in front of the tub, and then he pulled her up by her hair so her head hung over it. Then he looked at me like a wild animal."

"Do it, boy. Do it. Cut her neck while I got hold of her!' he yelled."

Linda's breath caught in her throat as the man's grip tightened, his fingers digging into her scalp like talons. With a sickening crack, her back arched in agony, the pain shooting through her body like bolts of lightning. She fought against his iron grip, desperation lending her strength, but it was futile. He was a beast, relentless and unforgiving.

In her mind's eye, she saw the boy with the knife, his eyes gleaming with madness, his hands eager to spill her blood. She knew what was coming, the blade slicing through flesh and bone, the searing pain that would follow. Her heart pounded in her chest, a drumbeat of terror echoing in her ears.

"I didn't want to do it, but I remembered what Daddy said. This wasn't a lady. It was a hog, a demon hog or something, and it was playing tricks on me. So I reached under her neck with that knife and pulled it as hard as I could across it."

Linda's world spiraled into darkness as the cold blade sliced through her flesh, a searing pain erupting from her throat. Blood gushed from the wound, a crimson torrent that choked her, drowning her in its iron embrace. Desperation clawed at her, but her lungs filled with blood, suffocating her stealing away her final breath.

With a feeble gasp, Linda fought against the darkness, her vision blurring as the world faded to black. The icy touch of death enveloped her, pulling her into its icy embrace. Her body went limp, her strength ebbing away with each passing moment.

As her head was forced down onto the unforgiving surface, Linda's consciousness slipped away, consumed by the void. The agony of her final moments echoed in the silence, a haunting lament lost to the night. And then, there was nothing but the stillness of death, a final, merciful release from the torment of the living.

"Daddy held her head down in the tub. After a minute, she stopped thrashing around and lay still. Blood got all over my hands and the tub, but hardly any got on the floor. She pissed some, but Daddy said that was a small mess compared to how bad it could've been."

"I looked at Daddy, and he was smiling at me. I knew I did well."

"Your grandpa would've been proud of you. You did that as well as any man could, but that part was easy. The hard part's cleaning them out and cutting them up."

"Daddy was right. He showed me how to do it. Damn, that first time was pretty rough on me. Like I said earlier, the smell is awful. It almost makes you not want to eat pork again, but eventually, we got the job done."

"Daddy showed me how to clean our tools in the tub because Momma wouldn't let us do it upstairs in the kitchen sink. She said it was unsanitary."

"We ended up with two bags of guts, a head, and the license plates to one of Daddy's trucks to get rid of. Daddy and I talked all the way to the pond. He must have told me a hundred times how proud he was. It made me feel pretty damn good about myself for the first time in I don't know when."

"We sat together for quite a while, looking out over the pond. I couldn't help but wonder what my momma's spirit was up to down at the bottom. Was she just lying in the mud or swimming around, waiting for someone to jump in? Or did she leave there and go to other places now and again? It was a mystery I figured I would never solve."

"While deep in thought, Daddy smacked me on the shoulder. I just about screamed. I was so caught up in thinking about my momma's spirit that I forgot Daddy was beside me. He had a good laugh about that."

"What's the matter, boy? Did I scare you?"

"I could have socked him in the nose, but I knew better. So, instead, I stood up like I was ready to go back to the house. 'Yes, you scared me."

"He was still laughing at me when he got to his feet. 'Well, boy, that's what happens when you get daydreaming,' he said."

"We started back to the house, with Daddy still laughing. That was when I heard a splash from the pond."

"Daddy and I both turned around just in time to see a naked boy about my age climbing out from the opposite side of the pond. He didn't look back at us. He just picked up his pile of clothes, ran straight into the cattails, and disappeared. We both stood there for a minute. Neither one of us was sure what to think."

"I finally asked Daddy, 'Who the hell was that?"

"Daddy kept his eye on the far shore. 'I don't know, boy, but I think it's time we get back to the house."

"We're just going to leave without looking for him?' I asked."

"Daddy glanced at me, then back to where the boy climbed out. 'We don't need to go looking for him. He'll be looking for us soon."

"I didn't know what to say, so I didn't say anything. After a few silent moments, he started back toward the house with me close behind."

"Before we went up the porch steps, Daddy leaned in close and warned me not to bring up what we just saw to Momma. He said there was no reason to get her fretting about something she couldn't control. I agreed not to say a word."

"That night, Momma made us a roast from the hog we killed earlier. I have to admit it was the best I'd ever had. I guess it was because I had a hand in it, and also, as I said before, Momma was the best cook I ever knew."

"Momma and Daddy tucked me into bed that night. Both of them were all smiles. I got a kiss from each one of them. The only strange thing was that Momma didn't sing to me that night. I felt a little hurt, but I guessed it was because I was a man now, and mommas don't sing to men. I admit I still cried a little, but I covered my head with my pillow so Momma and Daddy wouldn't hear."

"Before I went to sleep, I remember thinking, once I kill Momma, there won't be any bedtime singing or home-cooked meals."

Things that bump in the Night

"I woke up late that night; I'm not sure why. But I heard the strangest sound when I tried to go back to sleep. It was coming from downstairs. It was a kind of scraping sound, real soft-like. Kind of like someone walking in house slippers and not wanting anyone to hear them."

"I tried covering my head with pillows, but you know how that goes. Your air gets all hot, so you can hardly breathe. So I just lay there, listening. Whatever it was, it kept scraping really softly. It sounded like it was somewhere near the bottom of the stairs."

"I heard a creak. I knew that creak. It was the bottom step. Someone or something was sneaking up the stairs. I could hear it creeping slowly, step by step. I knew the top step was louder than the bottom, so I sat still and listened. Sure as shit, I heard it creak loud and long, like whoever it was, was heavy. I slid down in my blankets, so just my eyes were sticking out and stared at my door."

"Things were quiet for a while. I thought maybe I imagined the whole thing. Then there it was again. It was heading straight to my door. I was afraid to cry out for Daddy because I wasn't sure if it knew I was there. I thought whoever was there would go away if I lay quiet. But the footsteps continued."

"The door opened slowly, squeaking like always, but no one came in. Then, from under the door, I saw blood. It was pooling like whoever was behind it was bleeding terribly."

"Then I saw her. It was the magic hog from that morning. Her hair was a mess, and she looked pissed off. She was bleeding all around her neck, where I cut her, and dripping all over the floor. The tape was hanging off her face so I could see her eyes and mouth. She growled at me like some kind of animal, showing all her teeth, and each one was sure as shit hog's teeth all twisted this way and that."

"She just stared at me for a second, then knelt and started crawling slowly toward the foot of my bed, sniffing at the floor like she was tracking something. I was so scared I couldn't move."

"When she got to where I couldn't see her behind my footboard, I could feel the bed move a little. She was crawling under it. That's when I shot like a rocket straight up and out of that bed. I didn't even look back. I ran top speed to my daddy's room, hollering like I was on fire or something."

"I guess I must have scared the holy living shit out of my momma and daddy 'cause they both screamed, and Daddy damn nearly shot my head off. See, he kept an ole .38 next to his bed, and when I came running in, he let a round go in my direction. All I saw was a flash in the dark; then, I was blind because of the light. My head smacked into the wall on Momma's side of the bed. Before I could even see straight, Daddy slapped me around, yelling."

"What the fuck is your problem, boy? Are you trying to get yourself killed or something?"

"I was crying and trying to tell him some lady was under my bed, but he wasn't having any of it."

"He grabbed me by my shirt and dragged me back to my room, with Momma following right behind."

"Daddy was hollering. There ain't no goddamn lady under your bed, you dumb son of a bitch."

"He threw me down onto my bed, then he took that gun, put it tight to the side of my head, and said, 'Don't come running into my room like that again, or I'll kill you, you hear me? You're too old to be acting like that. You have a bad dream; you deal with it. You don't see me running around the house when I have bad dreams, do you?"

"No, Daddy,' I said.

"That is because I'm a man, not some chicken shit, little bitch. So now you better act like a man, or I'll get rid of you."

"Daddy took the gun from my head and walked out of the room, grabbing Momma by her arm as he left."

"I heard their door slam shut, and just like that, I was alone. I just kind of lay there in shock. It didn't make sense for Daddy to act like that and say those kinds of things after what we saw at the pond earlier. It didn't make sense."

"I knew he was more than just a little worried about what we saw. So much so that he made me promise not to tell Momma, and now he tells me I just had a bad dream. Regardless, there wasn't much I could do about it, so I decided to let the whole damn thing go and try not to think about it."

"Before long, I felt that damn hog lady under my bed again, bumping gently like she didn't want me to know she was there. I cried most of the night, but nothing else happened, and that hog lady didn't bother me other than moving around from time to time."

"It's funny, Dr. Creed, but I think she's still under that bed to this day. I say that because, for the rest of my days in that old house, I'd see her from time to time. She did nothing, just looked at me from under my bed, all pissed off. She didn't scare me much, either. I guess I got used to her being there as I got older."

Jacob

"Things were a lot different around the house after that. Momma and Daddy talked to me more like a grown-up, and they didn't take any shit from me either. If I did something childlike, well, then they'd beat the hell out of me, sometimes really bad."

"I remember this one time. It was right before my tenth birthday. I was playing out front, like kids do, when I saw a little boy sitting in one of Daddy's old cars. He was sitting on the driver's side, turning the steering wheel back and forth, and making car noises as if he were driving."

"I couldn't figure out where he could've come from. The nearest neighbors lived well over a mile away, and I was pretty sure they didn't have any kids. Then I thought he had to be the boy me and Daddy saw getting out of the pond."

"I walked up kinda slow like I didn't want to scare him away. So I opened the passenger door real slow. I looked at him and said, 'Hey, where did you come from, boy? You're not supposed to play in Daddy's cars."

"He ignored me and kept making car noises. I looked around. Daddy wasn't anywhere to be seen, plus the weeds had grown tall. So I figured I'd be safe getting inside and playing for a bit."

"I got in the car, shut the door softly, and looked at the boy. He was wearing a green John Deere baseball cap, a black shirt, and blue jeans. He was barefoot, just like me, and I could tell his hair was blond like mine because I could see it coming out from the sides of his hat."

"I asked him, 'What's your name?'"

"He kept looking straight ahead and said, 'Jacob.'"

"I waited a second to see if he would ask me my name, but he was too focused on driving. So I finally said, 'My name is Zackary—Zackary Williams, and I live here. Say, were you the boy I saw swimming in the pond? Where are you from, boy?"

"He still didn't answer me. He just kept making those damn car sounds. I was about getting ready to tell him he better answer me when he stopped and turned to look at me."

"I about shit myself. It was me. That boy was my goddamn twin. I tried to grab hold of the door handle to get away from him, but I couldn't find it. I was too scared to take my eyes off him."

"You don't need to be afraid of me, Zackary. My name is Jacob. I won't hurt you. We're brothers, and soon we will be really good friends."

"It was like looking in the mirror. He even had a nasty scar on his lip like me."

"I don't know why, but I said, 'I've got to go. I can't play right now—"

"Jacob suddenly glanced over my shoulder and said, 'You better hurry, Zack. Daddy's coming!"

"I turned around, and sure enough, Daddy was running across the porch, looking right at me. I opened the car door but wasn't fast enough to escape. Daddy kicked me hard in the back. I fell to the ground and curled up. After that, he laid into me. I felt the first few punches, and then I was out."

"Sometime later, I woke up. I could hardly see anything because my eyes were damn near swollen shut. But from what I could see, I knew I was in the cellar with my hands tied up over my head, hanging in the pigpen."

"I looked around, but no one was there except for that boy Jacob. He was standing by the stairs, looking up toward the living room. He was kinda lit up by the lights above."

"I whispered, 'Look what you did. Now I'm going to get beat real bad or even killed. I told you I'm not allowed in Daddy's cars."

"Jacob walked to the pen and whispered, 'Daddy's not gonna kill you."

"I wasn't too sure about that at all. 'Well, how do you know? Nothing has come out of this pen and stayed alive for long."

"Jacob smiled. 'Because you're his boy. He ain't going to kill his boy."

"Well, he killed you. He buried you while you were still alive."

"Zack, I wasn't his boy. I was just something he wanted to get rid of."

"Well then, he's going to beat the hell out of me. I know that for sure."

"If he does, you go somewhere else in your mind, Zack. You think about anything but what he's doing to you."

"That is some stupid shit you're saying, Jacob. How am I supposed to do that?"

"Jacob looked back at the stairs. 'Try, Zack."

"I closed my eyes because they were stinging so badly. When I opened them, Jacob was gone, but I heard Daddy creaking down the stairs. He was wearing his slaughtering apron. I knew then that he was going to kill me. He walked straight to the toolbox and slammed it down beside the tub. Then he opened it up and pulled out the keys."

"I asked him, 'Daddy, what are you going to do to me? I'm sorry for going in your car."

"Daddy didn't say a word. He just unlocked the door, then my hands. I thought he was going to let me walk out, but he grabbed me by the hair and pulled me out, just like he did to the hogs. The next thing I knew, he forced my head down into that goddamn tub. I could hear him fishing around inside the toolbox with his other hand, then he pulled my head back and put that cold knife against my throat."

"I felt him cut my skin a little. I tried crying out for Momma, but the knife cut a little each time my throat moved. Daddy held me like that for a while before he said, 'Next time I catch you in one of my cars, I'm going to kill you like a hog, and then I'll throw your body in the pond. You got it?'

"He let up on the knife so I could talk."

"I won't ever go near them again, I promise."

"Daddy took the knife from my neck, and just as he stood up, he dragged it deep across my back. I don't think he meant to cut me as badly as he did. He only wanted to teach me a lesson, not kill me after all, but he almost did."

"I knew it was bad because I felt the blade hang up on my spine, and there was a lot of blood down my back and legs. Daddy laid me facedown in the tub and hollered for Momma to get her sewing kit. I guess I must have passed out because I don't remember anything else after that."

"When I woke up, I was lying in my bed, hurting bad, and Jacob was sitting at the foot of my bed. He was concerned. I remember asking him, 'Am I going to die?'

"He smiled at me and said everything would be all right, and I believed him."

"I spent the next two weeks laid up in bed. Momma would come in now and again to feed me or wash my back, but I spent most of my days getting to know Jacob. We talked about everything. We liked all the same things, and he never called me awful names or anything like that. One night, I was lying in bed, and Jacob was on the floor in his usual spot. I remember it being pretty late, and I didn't feel like talking, but Jacob did."

"Zack, are you awake?"

"He knew I was. There was no need even to try to act like I wasn't. 'Yeah, I'm awake. What's the matter?'

"Well, nothing is wrong. I just want to talk to you about a few things."

"Like what?' I knew he would tell me whether or not I asked."

"You asked me a while back if I was the boy you saw swimming in the pond. Well, the truth is, it was me."

"He got my attention then. 'I figured it had to be you. There aren't any other kids anywhere near here. Why would you want to swim around in the pig pond anyway?"

"I wasn't just swimming. I was visiting our Momma, our real Momma."

"I rolled over and looked at him. 'So you know about our real Momma? Daddy told me all about her and how Grandpa killed her. At least that's what he told me, but he was lying. Our real Momma told me the truth, and he did it.' Momma told me you asked about it. She said she thought you should know the truth."

"Oh, I know the truth. And trust me, Jacob, once I get big enough, I'm going to kill him for doing that. He ruined my life. That should have never happened. Our real Momma and daddy should have raised us together."

"I agree, Zack. Momma won't leave until she feels like she's gotten revenge. She thought about trying to scare him off the property, but she knows he is bat-shit crazy. So scaring him away wouldn't work."

"That's even more reason why I'm going to kill him and Momma too."

"Good, Zack. They both need to go, and if they try sticking around here with the rest of us, I'll make them miserable."

"I wasn't sure what Jacob meant. 'What do you mean by the rest of us?"

"Zack, I'm talking about me, Momma, Daddy, the lady under the bed, and a bunch more."

"Are you talking about ghosts?"

"That's what I'm talking about. None of us want them around here."

"I looked around the room. I was feeling a bit uneasy, knowing a bunch of ghosts were running around."

"Zack, tonight Grandma will be in the cellar. She's been wandering around the yard looking for Grandpa. I talked with her. I told her I would open the freezer and let him out, but only if she and Grandpa leave and never come back."

"I never saw my grandma.' Yet, for some reason, I wanted to see her."

"That's a good thing, Zack. That bitch was every bit as evil as Momma and Daddy. But unfortunately, it runs in the family."

"For some reason, I always thought she was a nice lady, maybe like a normal grandma."

"How did she die, Jacob?"

"You'll see tonight. She should be showing up anytime now."

"I sure as hell didn't like the idea of Grandma showing up. 'Well, Jacob, I don't think—"

"There was a slow creak coming from downstairs. I knew the sound. It was the front door."

"Jacob stood up. 'Come on, Zack. You're going to open the freezer door for me."

"Hell no, I'm not opening the freezer door for you. I'm not leaving this room. You can handle your ghost business by yourself."

"That pissed Jacob off a little. 'Zack, now you listen to me. You are coming with me, and you're going to open the freezer. I've got to set Grandpa off on his way."

"There was no need to argue about it. I got up and followed Jacob. When we got downstairs, I noticed the front door was open. I thought, Why the hell do I have to open the freezer door? Obviously, Grandma opened the front door, so she shouldn't have a problem with the freezer."

"Jacob must have read my mind. 'She isn't allowed to open the freezer door. I won't let her."

"I didn't respond. The house was so damn quiet. I was afraid I would wake Momma and Daddy if I started talking."

"When we got to the cellar stairs, Jacob walked straight into the darkness. There was no way I would go down there with Grandma's ghost roaming around. So, I figured that was the perfect excuse not to get involved in this bullshit. However, Jacob outsmarted me by turning on one of the lights. He looked at me from around the corner."

"Hurry up, Zack. Get down here."

"I didn't have a choice, but I took it extra slowly, creeping down those damn stairs. When I finally reached the bottom, there was Grandma. She had a rope cinched around her neck, and her head was cocked to one side. Now I knew how Grandma died; she hanged herself. She had her hair pulled up and was wearing a filthy nightgown. Her bare feet looked like she hadn't worn shoes in a long time. She didn't seem to give a shit about seeing me. She just stood there, facing the freezer."

"I guess Jacob had enough of my staring. 'Zack, open the freezer.'"

"He kind of startled me. I half forgot he was there. I unlatched the freezer door, and just as I started to open it, it flew out of my hands, slamming into the wall. Grandpa sat straight up. He glanced at me before reaching a hand out to Grandma. She helped him climb out of there, leaving his body behind."

"Jacob walked to the stairs and pointed upward. 'Now go, both of you, and never come back."

"They didn't argue. They walked straight past Jacob and up the stairs, followed by Jacob. I shut the freezer door and followed them to the front door. Then, just like that, they walked away into the woods."

"I didn't wait for Jacob. I went straight into my room and hid under my covers. If Daddy hadn't

heard that freezer door slam, he must have been in one hell of a deep sleep. Still, I wasn't going to take any chances of getting caught having anything to do with it."

"Jacob came up a few minutes later. He laid down in his spot, just like nothing ever happened. 'Good night, Zack."

"I wasn't happy. I sat up. 'What do you mean good night? You got me running around here in the middle of the night helping you do some kind of exorcism shit, and just like that, you're ready to go to sleep?'"

"Jacob sighed like I was bothering him or something. 'Well, what do you want to talk about?'"

"Well, for one thing, I would like to know if Grandma hanged herself."

"Jacob rolled over so he was facing me. 'Yes, she hanged herself. From what the older ones told me, she wasn't raised the same way as Grandpa. She just got wrapped up in the killing until it was normal to her. I guess she liked it. She messed with the wrong person, though. Grandpa took a fourteen-year-old girl named Mary while she was walking home from school. No matter how much they beat her, she always tried to find a way to run back home. One day, Grandma snapped. She caught Mary trying to sneak out the front door, so she grabbed hold of her by the neck and strangled her. Well, Mary came back, and she was pissed. She haunted this house so damn bad that Grandma walked out back and ended it. Grandpa found her in the woods. He cut her down and buried her under the same tree."

"I was scared. I didn't want Mary messing with me, so I asked, 'Is Mary still here?'"

"No, she left right after Grandma hanged herself. She said she was going back to her house to be near her mom."

"Well, what about Momma and Daddy? Where were they when all this was going on?"

"They were just little ones, so Grandpa had to raise them by himself."

"I laid back down. I had heard enough. 'Okay, Jacob, I don't need to hear any more about it."

"Okay, Zack, good night."

"Jacob was right. We became good friends. Other than that damn hog lady bumping around under my bed all night, things were pretty good for a while."

"I never told Momma or Daddy about Jacob. I wanted to, but Jacob told me not to. He said they'd try to make him go away if I told them. I didn't want that. Jacob was the nicest thing I ever had in my life. Whenever Momma or Daddy would beat me, Jacob was there. I always kept my eyes on him while they were at it for whatever they said I did wrong. Jacob said they couldn't hurt me much as long as I did that, and he was right. Oh, sure, there were times I'd cry out. But mostly, that was just to get them to stop. See, I figured they enjoyed hearing me cry when they were hurting me."

"Well, as the years passed, I got a few fresh scars from Momma and Daddy. But other than that, life went on as usual."

The Field Trip

"I woke up to Jacob standing at the bedroom window, both hands on the frame, leaning forward like he was searching for something. I wasn't sure what the hell he could be looking for, but living in that house always came with surprises. So I figured I should get up and find out what had him so concerned."

"He glanced back at me when he heard the bed squeak, then back to the window. Not even a good morning. Whatever it was, it must have been pretty damn important."

"When I got to the window, I looked in the same direction he was. I didn't see anything other than the woods. 'Jacob, what are you looking for?"

"Jacob looked at me, eyebrows furrowed. 'I'm not looking for anything,' he said, returning his gaze to the window. 'I woke up earlier with a funny feeling. I can't describe it. I just knew something was wrong."

"'I get it,' I told him. 'But I usually feel the same things you do, and I didn't feel anything."

"I already told you. I can't describe it. It was just a funny feeling. So after breakfast, we're going for a walk."

"I looked at him like he was crazy. 'A walk? Where the hell are we going to go?"

"I'm taking you to where Daddy killed our family."

"I didn't know why he felt the need for us to go there, but I was curious about the place. So I wasn't going to argue. 'What are we going to tell Momma and Daddy? You know they're going to want to know what I'm up to."

"You're just going to tell them you're going out to play. Simple as that. We don't have far to go anyway. We'll be back before you know it."

"I knew better than that. I was sure Jacob and I would get into some trouble either on the way out there or back. There wasn't a day around here where something didn't get screwed up. But I figured if I didn't get an ass beating for being out too long, I would get one for some other kind of bullshit."

"Momma was up. I heard her down in the kitchen, clanging pots and pans around. It wouldn't be long before she hollered for me to eat breakfast. Daddy walked heavy-footed past my door."

"Momma's racket in the kitchen must have woken him up. I looked at Jacob.

"Well, it sounds like everyone is up and about. Should we head down and eat real quick?"

"Jacob shook his head. 'No, let's wait until Momma hollers for you before we do that. She might think something is going on if you show up early. We have to make everything seem like any other morning."

"Jacob was always smart when making plans, and he was right. I never went downstairs in the morning until Momma called me. Sometimes, I wonder why Grandpa chose me instead of Jacob. I wasn't anywhere near as smart as him. He should have been chosen to live, not me. I turned out to be nothing but a dipshit. Hell, I couldn't even write my name until he came along. He even taught me how to read. He told me to never let on that I knew how. He was afraid Momma and Daddy might beat me for being smarter than them."

"I went ahead and walked back to my bed. That damn lady underneath tried grabbing hold of my foot. I was getting tired of that. I wasn't in the mood for her antics this morning, so I let her know."

"Would you stop doing that shit? You know damn well you aren't going to get ahold of me, and even if you did, what then? You wouldn't do anything, but let me go anyway."

"Jacob, still standing at the window, started laughing. That pissed me off a little."

"Jacob, it isn't funny. She does that shit all the time."

"Oh, Zack, don't worry about her. That's just what she does. She doesn't mean anything by it."

"I wasn't satisfied with what he said. 'Jacob, I know damn well these spirits and shit around here will listen to you if you tell them something. So do me a favor and tell her to knock it off. Or even better, tell her to find some other place to live besides under my bed."

"Jacob walked toward the bed, still smiling. He thought this situation was funny. I knew I was right about the other spirits listening to him because when he got to the side of the bed, I heard her slide further under the bed. I think she was afraid of him."

"You see, Zack, she's harmless. Her problem is she's still new to all this being dead stuff. She doesn't know how to make herself look different or anything. She's kind of, well, you could say she's kind of like a baby ghost."

"Jacob, I never heard of anything more ridiculous in all my life."

"Jacob, as usual, was patient. 'Zack, there is a lot you don't understand about the dead. I'll tell you this, though. She feels safe under your bed. She's still scared of the other ones who live here. Once she decides she's ready, she won't always stay under your bed. She'll start messing with the living and doing regular ghost stuff. For now, this is what she's comfortable with."

"I felt a little bad for acting the way I had toward her. She didn't want to be in this situation any more than I wanted her to. From that time on, even if she annoyed me, I didn't yell at her. I just let her do what baby ghosts do."

"It wasn't long before we heard Momma hollering. 'Zack, get your ass down here and eat, and, of course, Daddy yelled, 'Yeah, you little shit mouse. Get your ass down here."

You hear that, Jacob? Shit mouse. I swear he is the biggest idiot I have ever seen."

"Jacob shrugged. 'Well, he can't help it, and he isn't going to change. Now get down there and eat breakfast. I'll meet you on the porch when you finish."

"After breakfast, I went out to the porch. Jacob was waiting, still looking out toward the woods. I didn't want to startle him, so I spoke as I walked over to him."

"I'm all set, Jacob. I told Momma and Daddy I would be out playing most of the day. They didn't say anything about having to come back and check in. Momma just said, "Have fun."

"Jacob didn't look at me. He just started walking toward the tree line. 'Okay, Zack, let's take a little walk."

"I couldn't help but wonder how far a little walk was. After just a moment of hesitation, I followed behind. There wasn't any sort of trail, so I just stayed close to Jacob. I knew he wouldn't get us lost."

"We didn't get very far before; out of the corner of my eye, I saw something moving in between the trees. Whatever it was, it was going in the same direction we were. I stopped and looked that way, but I didn't see anything. So I figured maybe the shadows were playing tricks on me. We continued through the woods for a while before I saw it again. I didn't stop walking, but I told Jacob."

"Jacob, I think something is following us. I keep seeing it between the trees."

"Jacob glanced back at me. 'Someone is following us."

"I thought he would say more, but he kept walking, so I had to ask.

"Who the hell is it?'

"Jacob stopped walking and faced me. 'It's Momma. She's just keeping an eye on us."

"Which Momma?"

"Our real Momma. She knows where we're going. I talked to her about it last night while you were sleeping."

"That surprised me. I didn't know Jacob left the room last night. I couldn't imagine I would have slept through something like that."

"She came into our room last night?'

"Jacob laughed. 'No, she didn't come into our room. She doesn't like coming into the house. I went to the pond while you were sleeping, and we talked."

"I knew it was probably a stupid question, but I asked Jacob," 'Did you jump in and swim down to her, or did she come up out of there?"

"Jacob rolled his eyes at me." 'Sometimes I go in and talk to her, but most of the time, she floats up. I know when she needs to talk to me. It's just a feeling that comes over me. When you're dead, you'll see what I mean. Anyway, she told me our daddy was lost. I guess he's been wandering around the woods for a long time. She thinks he'll find a way back to where he was born to be closer to his family. She said he doesn't want any part of being stuck around here."

"That kind of made sense to me. I would do the same thing if I were a ghost. Still, I wondered why Daddy waited so long."

"I guess you can't blame him, Jacob. Is that why we're going to where he was killed?"

"That's one reason, but I know he's already gone. I felt him leave early this morning. Don't ask me to try explaining that, either. The other reason we're going is because Momma asked me to."

"So he isn't lost. He just left?"

"He was lost, but he found his way out and figured out a way to go home. Momma just doesn't know that for certain. She hasn't learned how to sense that yet. For me, it's natural. But, Zack, there is something I should tell you. I have a lot more power than any other spirits around here. I don't know why, but I do. The other ones either like me or fear me."

"I suspected as much, but I didn't know why. 'That's all interesting, Jacob, but if you're so powerful, why is Momma keeping an eye on us?"

"Jacob laughed. 'I already told you. That's just what good Mommas do, Zack. So I'll tell her to stop hiding and follow us so you can see her."

"Jacob waved his hand toward the trail behind us, but nothing happened. He looked at me and shrugged, then hollered out. 'Quit your hiding so Zack can see you."

"It took a minute or so, but Momma stepped out from behind a tree and walked toward us. I was surprised. She was wearing a dirty old white nightgown."

"Hey Jacob, would you have a look at that? She's not naked anymore."

"That's because I told her to find something to cover herself. I was tired of seeing her walking around with no clothes on."

"Where did she find the nightgown?"

"I don't know, probably at the bottom of the pond. I'm not going to get on Momma about it. Anything is better than seeing her naked."

"I couldn't help but wonder why she was naked in the first place. 'What happened to the clothes she had on when they threw her in the pond?"

"She didn't have any. For some reason, Grandpa and Daddy took all her clothes off and burned them before they tossed her in."

"That didn't make sense, but trying to figure out why Grandpa and Daddy ever did anything was impossible.

"I don't know if she was embarrassed because we knew she was following us or if she didn't like having to wear that old nightgown, but Momma took her sweet time catching up with us. When she did, Jacob said, 'Are you ready, Momma?' She nodded and followed behind me as Jacob led the way."

"Now, I know you shouldn't be too worried about your mom walking behind you, but Momma had a smell to her, like a dead coon or something. Plus, she wasn't breathing right; she sounded like she was trying to suck air through a straw. I have to admit, I did look over my shoulder at her a few times just to make sure she wasn't standing too close to me."

"After a while, we walked out into a small clearing. There was no sign of anyone ever having camped there remaining. Instead, tall weeds and thorn-laden blackberry bushes reclaimed the area. Jacob stopped before turning around toward Momma and me."

"This is where it happened."

"I think Momma already knew that. She walked past Jacob and me toward the center of the clearing. She pointed at a giant bramble of berry bushes without looking back at us."

"Jacob walked to her, and they stood there for several minutes, just staring. Jacob turned and looked at me. 'Momma says this is where she and Daddy were killed."

"I didn't know what to say. I just stood there looking around, trying to imagine the scene that took place many years ago."

"Jacob walked around Momma, then not more than ten feet into the woods, he stopped and stared at the ground. 'This is where Daddy and I are buried. They dug a hole, threw us in, and walked away like nothing happened. It's weird, Zack, but even though I was no more than two years old, I had this vision of a dark figure throwing dirt on me. I remember fear and confusion, and that's it. There is nothing else to the memory, just fear, confusion, and dirt."

"A chill went through my entire body when I thought about how it could have easily been me. But then again, I wouldn't exactly consider it luck. At least Jacob's torment ended that night. Unfortunately, mine has gone on for years. I had to walk away. The whole place felt heavy. Knowing what happened here made me want to start running."

"We stopped at what was likely once the road that led to the clearing. It was nothing more than a narrow strip of weeds and tree saplings that wound its way through the woods. I couldn't help but wonder why anyone unfamiliar with the area would venture out here to camp. Maybe it was because they were young and adventurous. I don't know. Whatever the reason, it cost them their lives. I had seen all I could handle for the day. I was ready to leave."

"I walked back to where Jacob was standing. 'Jacob, let's go home. I don't want to be here anymore."

"I don't either. Momma knows Daddy is gone.' He nodded toward Momma. 'See, she's leaving."

"I turned around, and sure enough, she had already started back the way we came."

Life Goes On

"Life went on. Momma was always cooking or cleaning. Me and Jacob would run around the yard playing. And once in a while, Daddy would make his runs into the city, usually staying out half the night, but that was what he liked to do. I asked him once if it would be easier if he picked up hogs in town, but Daddy said it was too close to home. He said the cops protected those bitches, and they'd catch on real quick if all of them started disappearing. So once every couple of months, he'd make his trip to the city, and I would help in the cellar when he got home."

"It got easy for me. The lady hogs couldn't trick me anymore. I could see right through them for what they were. I even learned to ignore all their crying and carrying on. Of course, they were just meat, and the family needed meat to survive, but I will admit there was this one that kind of got to me."

"I was seventeen when she came. It had been a boiling July, and that day was no exception. It had to be easily over ninety degrees. Daddy and I were out front, tinkering around on Grandpa's old truck. Earlier that morning, we figured we ought to give her a tune-up, so we ran into town and picked up some spark plugs and oil."

"There we were, out in the front yard, sweating like two hogs. I remember being so damn thirsty that I could hardly stand it. I thought about heading into the house for some water, but I knew that would set Daddy off on some pissed-off rant. So I was just working up my nerve when the front door squeaked open."

"When I looked up from under the hood, Momma walked out with two glasses of ice-cold water. Daddy couldn't see because he was finishing up under the truck, so I said, 'Daddy, come up out of there. Momma's bringing something to drink."

"Daddy slid out from under the truck, covered in grease and oil. 'Well, sweet Jesus, it's about time, Momma. We're about to die out here."

"Momma just laughed at him and gave us our glasses. I was so damn thirsty. I tilted mine straight back. I would have swallowed it all in one go, except I started choking. So, I got most of it on my shirt instead of where I wanted it to go. He and Momma started laughing at me while I tried to catch my breath. Finally, I turned away so they could just look at my back. That was when I heard Jacob standing at the corner of the house, almost like he was hiding."

"Zack, listen. Momma said a lady is walking up the road. Momma said she's hurt or something. Jacob pointed toward the driveway. 'I see her, Zack. She's coming."

"When I looked in the direction Jacob was pointing, I saw her too. She had pretty brown hair and wore a white tank top with blue shorts. I could tell she was pregnant because her belly was so big. She was walking right toward us. And she didn't look like she was feeling too well either. She was kind of swaying this way and that."

"Now, I had never seen anyone walk up that road. It was a good half-mile from the main highway and all uphill. The sight of her scared the shit out of me. I turned around and said, 'Momma, Daddy, shut your damn mouths. Look what's coming up the road."

The Abduction of Sarah Buchanan

Sarah Buchanan, twenty-four, looked down at the flat tire. "Shit," she said under her breath. She looked back in the direction she had come. There was nothing. The road stretched for a quarter-mile, disappearing behind a heavily wooded curve.

She looked in the opposite direction; other than a rusted mailbox leaning precariously backward and almost entirely hidden by wild blackberry vines, it was much the same. It was a quarter-mile stretch of road that disappeared around a sharp curve. She crossed her arms as she leaned back against her door.

Sarah tried using her cell phone several times. The surrounding woods and mountains blocked all reception in the area. But, she thought, someone had to drive by eventually, and no one would drive by an eight-month pregnant woman stranded on the side of the road without stopping to help.

Sarah looked down at her watch. Forty-five minutes had passed, and not a single car. The July heat and the humidity became unbearable as the hour approached noon.

"Why haven't I ever learned to change a flat tire?" she wondered miserably. The thing was, she should've known better. She was always teaching her first graders the importance of preparedness, yet here she was—unprepared.

A proverb surfaced in her head: "Shortcuts lead to long delays." Whoever thought of that one must have done something as stupid as I have, she thought. I could have taken Highway 30 from Little Creek to Ridge Rock, a very straight, well-used road. But no, I took a shortcut up Highway 1 a winding, rarely used road that runs straight through hillbilly country.

Sarah's gaze fell upon the mailbox, its open door an eerie invitation. Leaving her car, she ventured toward it. The mailbox held an unusual surprise; a fresh stack of junk mail, the epitome of unsolicited clutter. She stole a furtive look in both directions, confirming her solitude, and then seized the topmost flier from the pile. "Jimmy's Lube and Tube," it proclaimed. An enticing offer beckoned: an oil change for compact cars at the unbeatable price of $16.99. The deal was valid from Saturday, July 12, through Monday, the twenty-first. She noted that today was Friday, July 15; as she flipped through the other advertisements, she noticed each bearing current dates.

This revelation hinted that someone was keeping tabs on the mailbox, a subtle sign of local residents. Sarah nonchalantly returned the mail to its resting place and returned to her car. Retrieving her keys from the ignition, she glanced at her suitcase, resting innocently on the rear seat. It held nothing of significant value, just a selection of outfits for her impending three-day visit to her mother's home. She deliberated briefly before deciding it was safe to leave it behind. Locking her car doors, she cast another wary glance in both directions and then, with a hint of trepidation, started her journey up the desolate dirt road beside the mailbox.

The journey commenced with relative ease, a leisurely stroll along the road. However, the path soon transformed into a daunting ascent into the looming embrace of the thick, unforgiving forest ahead. Unforgiving rains had carved deep, treacherous ruts into the road's entire expanse, creating an arduous challenge for the intrepid traveler.

Sarah discovered that navigating the waist-high brambles adorning the road's flanks was less of an ordeal than struggling through the unforgiving ruts. As the day advanced, the oppressive heat intensified, mercilessly swathing her in moisture. Beads of sweat trickled down her spine and legs, a testament to her exertion. Seeking respite, she rested beneath the shade of a colossal pine tree. Her eyes sought solace on the road ahead. It seemed to plateau about fifty yards further - a glimmer of promise in her relentless journey. "A stroke of fortune," she whispered, though the deafening cicada chorus drowned her words. Still, no signs of humanity met her gaze, and the eerie silence of the woods prevailed, disturbed only by the relentless cicadas.

Undaunted, Sarah pressed on, her footsteps hastened by the road's newfound gentleness. The once-formidable ruts had lessened in their assault, allowing her to regain the shoulder of the road, transforming her trek into a more manageable ordeal.

Suddenly, her attention was seized by a peculiar sight. On the road's surface lay muddy footprints, as though marking the trail of an unseen traveler. But the impressions terminated abruptly, dissolving into perplexing ambiguity. An unsettling feeling gnawed at her senses. She gazed in every direction, perusing the dense woods and underbrush that embraced the road. The panorama revealed no signs of life, no lingering echoes of humanity. A sharp glance over her shoulder yielded only solitude. Nevertheless, an unshakable sensation settled upon her - the eerie certainty of unseen eyes watching her every move.

Sarah continued up the gnarled road while behind her, concealed in the forest depths, dead gray eyes stared at her with a hunger that could chill the devil himself to the bone.

The presence didn't make itself known—a shadowy figure lurking among the trees, its form obscured by the darkness. The woman's tattered gown swayed in the breeze, her hair dripping with water. Her unblinking gaze pierced through the trees, locking onto Sarha with a chilling intensity. For a moment, the world seemed to hold its breath, the silence broken only by the rhythmic hum of the cicadas.

A perplexing internal struggle wrestled within Sarah's mind. A part of her yearned to retreat to the safety of her car, while another, more resilient facet urged her onward, seeking salvation on this desolate road. The road behind her held the shadows of potential danger, and the thought of unseen eyes tracking her every move sent shivers down her spine. What if the peril was behind her? What if the unseen observer was merely biding its time, waiting for the perfect moment to strike?

Despite the gnawing uncertainty, Sarah's resolve hardened, and she increased her pace, casting frequent glances over her shoulder. The canopy of trees lining the road began to recede, revealing an expanse of land. This was her beacon, the harbinger of potential safety or aid.

Her steps slowed as a distant sight emerged on the horizon - a house. An aging, two-story white structure, visibly marred by time's relentless touch. Yet, for Sarah, it represented the sliver of hope she so desperately sought. The crumbling house appeared abandoned, a lighthouse in the sea of wilderness.

As she drew closer, a motley assortment of derelict vehicles greeted her sight, their forms merging with the encroaching flora. Many were immobilized, missing wheels, propped on blocks, or resting on their axles. These decrepit automobiles became makeshift islands amid the sea of overgrown weeds, their rusted roofs defying the relentless forces of decay. But one anomaly stood amidst this mechanical graveyard, a battered Chevy pickup truck. Its hood remained open, awaiting, perhaps, the cannibalized remnants of other vehicles to ensure its own survival.

Sarah approached the residence, her weary steps growing heavy. Ahead, she spied three figures, two men and a woman. A wave of hope surged within her, and she waved in their direction. To her dismay, they appeared oblivious to her presence, locked in their own world. Sarah pressed onward, her fatigue compelling her to reach the end of this surreal journey.

The closer she drew to the trio, the more they resembled archetypal hillbillies, the kind of people one might expect to find living in the heart of nowhere. The woman's imposing frame, standing at around six feet, bore the physicality of a man. She donned a handcrafted flower-print dress, with her brown hair tightly bundled into a bun.

The man, presumably the woman's husband, loomed over six feet tall, a veritable behemoth, his physique resembling that of a lumberjack. His unruly, jet-black hair matched the wild tangle of his beard, obscuring much of his face.

The third individual, significantly younger, bore the semblance of their offspring, and Sarah pegged him as their son. Towering above six feet in height like his parents, he sported a disheveled mane of shoulder-length, sun-kissed blond hair. His attire consisted solely of a pair of weathered, knee-torn blue jeans.

The first to lock eyes with Sarah was the youngest of the trio. He pointed in her direction, alerting the others to her presence. Sarah observed an exchange of words between the father and son before the youthful man abruptly turned and darted into the house. An unsettling unease crept over her, whispering that something was amiss. Yet, it was too late to retreat. The die was cast, and she understood that these enigmatic denizens of the wilderness would not permit a stranger to venture up their road and then simply vanish without explanation.

Sarah pressed on, a strained smile adorning her face. The trio returned her gesture with smiles of their own. She dared to hope that things might be alright in this peculiar encounter.

"Daddy squinted his eyes and looked down the road before he grabbed my arm. 'Boy, go hide. You'll scare her away if she sees you all marked up like you are. Now go on. Go up in your room till I call you."

"I figured he was right. I got this scarred-up lip, and I wasn't wearing a shirt, so you could see where Momma had stitched me up and all the other marks crisscrossing me from the other beatings. So I went. I ran straight up the stairs and into my room."

"Jacob was already there, staring out my window. I pushed him out of the way so I could see. He didn't like that."

"Zack, you shouldn't push me like that. I never push you around, do I?"

"I moved over a little so that he could see too. Jacob stood beside me, and we watched the whole thing play out. She walked right up to where Momma and Daddy were standing. The lady looked really hot. Her face was red, and she was all sweaty. I watched Momma put her arm around her and walk her toward the house. I think the lady saw me looking down at her because she looked up at me for a second just before they stepped onto the porch."

"I can't explain, but I knew this lady was special. I was hoping to get a look at her before Daddy killed her. Part of me was hoping Daddy wouldn't have to kill her."

"When they walked into the house, Jacob went to my door and listened to them talking. I couldn't hear what Momma was saying, but I could tell she was talking sweetly to the lady. Daddy was too. The lady didn't sound like she was worried about anything. At least she wasn't hollering like she was."

"After a bit, I just lay on my bed and waited for Daddy to come up and get me."

As Sarah approached the couple, the woman bestowed upon her a gap-toothed grin, her mouth showcasing a conspicuous absence of dental fixtures. Darleen waved a callused hand and asked, "Well, girl, what the hell are you doing up here?"

Sarah mustered a nervous smile. "I'm sorry for trespassing on your property, but I got a flat down on the highway and don't know how to fix it. I thought maybe I could find someone to help me or use a phone."

Observing Charlie stealing a glance over her shoulder toward the road, Sarah detected an undercurrent of unease. "You say you came all the way up from the highway?" he asked.

"Yes, sir, but if you want me to leave, I will. I don't want to cause any problems."

"Are you by yourself, girl?" he asked, his gaze again drawn to the road.

Sarah hesitated. She had no desire to divulge her solitary status, but she couldn't concoct a believable story about her invisible carload of friends, deciding that the pregnant woman should embark on a half-mile hike through the woods for help. "Yes, sir, just me. And I'll tell you, that was one heck of a walk, especially when you're carrying this in front of you." Sarah gently patted her burgeoning belly, hoping her pregnant state might garner some sympathy if these people turned out to be unusual.

Charlie squinted, casting a discerning eye upon Sarah's midsection. "What's your name, girl?"

"Sarah, Sarah Buchanan. I'm a first-grade math teacher at Little Creek Elementary. I was on my way to Ridge Rock to visit my mom for a few days when my tire blew out."

Charlie donned his best facade, a saccharine smile stretched wide across his tooth-depleted grin. Sarah noted that his dental situation mirrored his wife's.

"Well, Miss Sarah, I ain't never heard of no Little Creek Elementary, but that doesn't make no matter to me. You're welcome here. My name's Charlie, and this is my wife, Darleen."

Darleen chimed in, casting a welcoming aura as she encircled Sarah with her arm. "Now, baby doll, come into the house out of this heat while I get you something cool to drink."

Feeling constrained and not entirely in control, Sarah obediently followed Darleen towards the front door, like a child being led by the hand. Just before ascending the steps, Sarah noticed movement above her. She looked up and met the gaze of the young man, his eyes devoid of expression, who seemed to be watching her from an upstairs window. Then, as they crossed under the porch roof and entered the house, he vanished from her sight.

Sarah's eyes darted around the interior, observing the antiquated yet impeccably maintained furniture. She couldn't help but think that some of these pieces might fetch a fortune. Black-and-white photos adorned the walls, presumably family portraits, all captured in front of this very house. The individuals in the photographs shared an uncanny familial resemblance and bore the same vacant expressions, staring back at her with dead eyes. To Sarah, it was a rather homely family.

Darleen and Charlie ushered her into the kitchen, seating her at an elegant oak table. Although relieved to escape Darleen's grasp, Sarah couldn't shake the feeling that she had unwittingly walked into a spider's lair.

Darleen offered a reassuring pat on her shoulder and inquired, "Baby doll, you sit right there while I get some lemonade. Does that sound good, honey?"

Sarah hesitated, her unease manifesting in her voice. "That would be great, ma'am, especially after that walk. I didn't know your house was so far from the road."

Charlie settled across from Sarah at the table, grinning from ear to ear as he began to speak. "It's a long way. We ain't never, and I mean never, had no one walk up that road. We've had kids come up looking for a place to booze her up from time to time, but that's about it. I usually run out with my shotgun, acting all crazy and shit. That gets them hightailing it right the hell out of here quicker than greased lightning." Charlie erupted into laughter.

Sarah couldn't help but notice the sorry state of his teeth, stained a foul yellow with spots of black. She averted her gaze and managed a polite chuckle. "Oh, you watch your mouth, Daddy. No need for this pretty young thing to hear your swearing mouth," Darleen scolded.

Sarah smiled politely and surveyed the room for a phone, finding none. When she raised her gaze, she met Charlie's suspicious stare. "What are you looking for, Miss. Sarah?"

In her sweetest tone, Sarah replied, "Oh, nothing, sir. I was just looking around, admiring how nice your home is. I love all your antique furniture."

A venomous retort accompanied Charlie's nod. "Now, just what the fuck is that supposed to mean? This house and all the stuff here have been around for over a hundred years, and we like it. All of it."

Sarah felt a shiver creeping down her spine. Charlie had misinterpreted her innocent comment. "I apologize. Everything is beautiful. I didn't mean to offend you, sir," she said, her voice quivering.

Charlie continued scrutinizing her across the table, a potential threat looming in his eyes. At Darleen's request, they briefly excused themselves, their hushed conversation in the other room hinting at tension. Sarah contemplated the room's layout, briefly glancing at the front door.

The urge to flee was overwhelming, but she knew the peril of attempting to outrun these apparent lunatics, especially when unfamiliar with the area and heavily pregnant. She concluded that it was time to forgo pleasantries and request the use of their phone, prepared to leave with or without their assistance.

Charlie and Darleen reentered the room, both wearing unnervingly pleasant smiles. Sarah sensed the underlying tension but decided to feign ignorance. Charlie, extending his filthy hand, approached Sarah with a broad smile. "Miss Sarah, I hope you will forgive my swearing mouth. I don't know what came over me."

Sarah forced a strained smile while shaking Charlie's hand, trying to hide her aversion to his leather-like skin.

"It's okay, sir. You didn't offend me," she replied.

Charlie grinned. "Well, just the same, I am sorry," he said, then turned to Darleen. "Momma, I'm going to run upstairs and get that lazy boy of yours."

"Ain't my boy. He's yours," she chuckled.

Seated too close for comfort, Darleen made Sarah feel uneasy, though she discreetly attempted to avoid the unpleasant scent of Darleen's breath.

Darlene flashed a smile. "Now, baby, we can have some lady talk."

"About an hour had passed when Jacob suddenly yelled, 'Zack, Daddy's coming!' Then he ran off into the closet. I don't know why he did that. He knew damn well nobody could see him but me."

"I sat up in my bed, and sure enough, a few seconds later, Daddy came flying into the room looking pretty damn happy."

"Hurry, boy, put a shirt on. It seems the lady got herself a flat down the road. We gotta get that damn car before someone sees it."

"I jumped up and did as Daddy said."

"This isn't one of them lady hogs, boy. Miss Sarah's not from around these parts. She came all the way from Little Creek. She said she was going to her momma's place in town. So when we get downstairs, we just talk real nice. We have to be careful about what we say around her. We don't want to scare her, or she might try running off. If she does that, we'll have to kill her."

"I said, 'Okay, Daddy, I'll be nice."

"We walked downstairs, and there was Miss Sarah at the kitchen table, drinking a glass of lemonade. I could see how she looked at me. She noticed my lip right off but still smiled at me."

"Hello,' she said.

"Momma looked at me, glowing like an angel. 'Sarah, this is our son, Zackary. Zackary, say hi to Sarah."

"Hi,' I said, followed by an awkward silence. After that, I didn't know what else to say."

"Daddy laughed and said, 'Well, Miss Sarah, he ain't much for talking, but he's good with cars. So you just stay with Momma. We'll fix your car and bring her back here to you. How's that?'

"Oh no, that's okay. If I could just use your phone, my cell doesn't work out here, but I'll call Triple A. They'll send someone out."

"Well, honey, we don't have a phone,' Daddy said with a shrug. 'But it ain't no trouble for us to get your car for you."

"I think she was nervous about giving us her car keys, but she had no choice. So she handed Daddy the keys."

"Thank you. I don't mean to be such trouble."

"Oh, nonsense,' Momma said. 'Daddy and Zackary love working on cars. Now can I get you something else to drink, baby?' Momma started rubbing Miss Sarah's back like she used to do to me, smiling like this was the best day of her life."

"Daddy and I walked out the door. I could hear Momma laying it on real sweet and Miss Sarah sounding like she was buying every bit of it."

"Daddy poured the oil into the truck and slammed the hood down. When he hopped in the cab, he was so excited he could hardly stand it. He fired up the engine and started giggling away as we bumped down the road."

"Daddy, what's got you so wound up?' I asked."

"Daddy glanced over at me, all wild-eyed. 'Cause, boy, you see that woman is with child, right?"

"Yeah, Daddy."

"Well, your momma's been talking about wanting a baby girl."

"I wasn't sure what Daddy was talking about, so I said, 'So what?'"

"Well, you stupid shit, when he got to the car, re gonna take that woman's baby."

"Well, how do you know it's gonna be a girl, Daddy?"

"He slapped me across the mouth. 'You stop talking like you're so damn smart, you hear me? It just so happens your Momma knows things, and not more than a week ago, she had dreamed God gave her a baby girl. So now keep that shit mouth of yours shut if you don't got nothing good to say."

"I gritted my teeth. 'Sorry, Daddy, I didn't mean to talk no shit."

"Daddy was quiet for a minute, then he started giggling again like a crazy man. I ain't ever seen him act like that before."

"When we got to the highway, her car was sitting to the left of our driveway. It was one of those little blue Honda Civics, and as she said, the front tire was flat and half shredded."

"Daddy turned the truck around so we could park behind the Civic. He handed me the keys and said, 'Hurry, boy, get in it and get it off the road.' He was looking around all wide-eyed and nervous. Guess he was afraid someone would drive up on us."

"I jumped into the car and drove it, flat tire and all, straight up our driveway. That little car wasn't made for a torn-up old road like ours. It kept slamming and scraping along so badly that I didn't think I would make it all the way."

"Daddy was so close behind me that I thought he would run right up my ass. I suppose that was his way of saying he didn't care if the damn wheels fell off the car as long as I got it up to the house, which I did."

"When we pulled into the yard, Daddy jumped out of the truck and right at me with his pocketknife. I didn't know what the hell he had in mind, so I locked the doors. When he got to the car, Daddy motioned me to roll the window down. I did, but only a crack. He looked at me too wound up, and I didn't trust him. He glanced at the window. 'Hurry, boy, turn the wheel. I'm going to cut the brake lines."

"I did as he said, and he cut the driver's sidelines with his pocketknife. Then he stood up, rubbing his head like he was concerned by what he was looking at. 'Well, boy, it looks like we got more than a flat tire here. We got some shredded brake lines too."

"I got out and went along with his game. 'Well, whatever shall we do, Daddy?"

"We both laughed at how I said, 'Whatever shall we do?'

"When we went into the house, Daddy told Ms. Sarah about her car. She looked scared."

"I'm sorry to tell you this, but you have some torn-up brake lines along with your flat tire. My guess is it happened when that tire blew out. A piece probably shot up and cut them. Damn lucky Zack got her this far without wrecking her."

"I could tell Miss Sarah didn't believe a single word Daddy said, but all she said was, 'Do you think it would be okay if you drove me into town so I can make a phone call?"

"Daddy said he could do it, but first, he had to wash up and eat. He patted my shoulder and said, 'Let's wash up, boy. Momma, can you make something to eat real quick?'

"Momma smiled at Miss Sarah as she got up from her chair.

"Oh no, not at all, Daddy and Miss Sarah; you might as well have something, too."

"As Daddy and I walked down to the cellar to wash up, I heard Miss Sarah say she wasn't hungry. I could sense this was going to be a serious problem."

The unease in Sarah's gut grew stronger. She knew her car's brake lines weren't damaged when she left it. It had driven fine until the tire tore loose, making steering nearly impossible. The brakes had worked without a hitch then. Zackary, too, gave her the creeps. His gaze sent shivers down her spine, and his eyes appeared drained of life, like a zombie rather than a living person. His facial scars only amplified the eerie vibe. She decided she needed to leave as soon as the opportunity arose, even if it meant causing harm to one of them during her escape.

Sarah observed Darleen closely, waiting for the right moment to make her move. She hoped that Darleen would turn her back so she could run, but Darleen kept her in her line of sight, confirming Sarah's suspicions. Her heart raced as she watched Darleen step back from the counter where she was slicing tomatoes. Darleen reached into the refrigerator, retrieving a jar of mayonnaise. Sarah smiled as pleasantly as she could manage, trying not to reveal her anxiety.

"Oh, no mayo for me, ma'am," she said, pretending to be unaware of their true intentions.

Darleen's expression contorted as if Sarah had uttered something repulsive. "Well, the rest of us are having mayo, and you can't have a tomato sandwich without mayo. That'd be plain nasty."

Sarah forced a nervous laugh. "Alright, if everyone else is having mayo, I'll have some too."

Darleen grinned. "First time for everything, baby." She began spreading mayonnaise on the sandwiches, humming all the while and keeping her unwavering gaze fixed on Sarah.

"When we got to the cellar, Daddy said, 'Nobody's going to town, boy. We're just going back upstairs to see how this plays out. Don't do anything stupid.'"

"I wasn't planning on it unless Daddy said so, so I just said, 'Okay, Daddy.'"

"When we were done cleaning up, Daddy and I went back upstairs, pretending like nothing was amiss. Momma had prepared some lovely tomato sandwiches, and she was all smiles. I hoped she'd stay that way, but I knew it wouldn't last long."

"Now, Miss Sarah, we're all going to enjoy a nice lunch, and then Zackary will drive you to town. Does that sound alright, darling?" Momma asked.

"That's fine, but I'd like to get to a phone before it gets too late."

"That was when Daddy snapped for a second. He slammed his fist on the table, rattling all the dishes, and yelled, 'Now listen here, goddamn it. You've already been told we are going to have lunch first, and then we're going to take you into town."

"I looked at Miss Sarah. Her eyes got big like she was getting ready to scream or something."

"Daddy tried real quick to fix what he'd done by smiling and saying, 'Does that sound okay, darling?' But the damage was done."

"Miss Sarah stood up slowly, knocking her chair over, and said, 'I think I should go now.'"

"She tried walking to the front door, but Momma jumped up as quick as lightning. She grabbed hold of Ms. Sarah's hair. Poor Miss Sarah started kicking and screaming, but she was no match for Momma. Momma reached around Miss Sarah's neck with her arm and started squeezing.

Daddy and I jumped to help Momma, but she didn't need us. She made Miss Sarah go limp pretty fast."

"See, Doctor, if you get hold of someone right around the neck, you can stop all the blood from going up into their brain. They can still breathe, but they just go to sleep without blood. Daddy taught me how to do it when I was a kid. He even let me practice on some of them lady hogs. I got so damn good at it that I could grab hold of one of them hogs and choke them out before they had time to do anything."

"Get hold of her feet, Daddy. We're going to run her up to Zack's room. Zack, go down to the cellar and get daddy's rope. Hurry, boy!' yelled Momma."

"I ran as fast as I could, and when I came back up, Momma and Daddy were already at the top of the stairs, going into my room. I could see Ms. Sarah was coming around because her legs were starting up again, and Daddy was hollering."

"Hurry the fuck up with that rope, you worthless piece of shit!"

"I ran up the stairs and into my room. Daddy held Miss Sarah's legs on my bed while Momma was choking her again. Daddy took the rope from me and tied Miss Sarah tight to the bed. Then he said to Momma, 'Well, what the fuck do you want me to do? If I cut her open up here, she's going to make a mess all over the goddamn place."

"We ain't going to do no cutting. Miss Sarah is going to have that baby any day now, so it would be best if we keep her alive,' Momma said."

"Without thinking, I said, 'Well, Momma, where am I supposed to sleep?"

"Momma's eyes flashed. I knew I fucked up."

"Now you listen to me, boy. You can see we got a lot going on around here. You keep running that stupid ass mouth of yours, and I swear I'll let Daddy hang you in the cellar."

"I backed away from her a bit toward my door. Then, I don't know what came over me. I said, 'I was just wondering where I was going to sleep, that's all."

"That was when Daddy hit me and sent me to the floor. Then he said, 'Don't you worry about where you'll sleep. You're lucky you even have a bed. Now get your stupid ass downstairs and start cleaning up."

"I was furious at Miss Sarah for taking my bed, but I didn't say a thing back to Daddy. I just did what he said. It wasn't long after I started cleaning up when I heard Miss Sarah come around. She was screaming and hollering. I could hear Momma and Daddy yelling right back. They told her to shut her fucking mouth. She kept it up until Momma laid into her.

"I heard Momma smack the shit outta Miss Sarah three or four times, maybe more, then I heard Momma yell, 'You make one more goddamn noise, bitch, and daddy will cut your throat right where you lie."

"That seemed to have worked because Miss Sarah went from screaming to sobbing. It wasn't long after that before Daddy came downstairs. He was happy again. He said, 'Boy, we have to get rid of that bitch's car before someone comes around and sees it."

"I nodded and asked what we were gonna do with it."

"We're going to take her round back to the shed. That little car is small enough. I can cut her up with my torch, and then we'll throw all the pieces deep down in the pond where I dump all the trash."

"I didn't like that idea much because I knew he meant I would be the one who took all the pieces to the trash pond, but I didn't argue."

"We spent most of the night cutting that car up. Finally, around two o'clock in the morning, I threw the last piece into the pond. Even Miss Sarah's suitcase went to the bottom. I was sure glad the job was done. I was so worn out that I didn't know how much longer I could have gone. So was Daddy. He said, 'Now if anyone comes poking around, we don't have to worry about them seeing that car. They ask about it; we'll just tell them we ain't seen nothing strange around here."

"Okay, Daddy. But where am I supposed to sleep tonight?' See, I'd been thinking about that since Daddy tied Miss Sarah to my bed. I just couldn't seem to take my mind off it.

"Goddamn you, boy. Did you hear what I was just saying about someone coming around here? Stop worrying about where you'll sleep and pay attention to what I'm telling you. If someone comes around, I don't want you talking to them. You just disappear. That way, you don't fuck anything up, you hear me?'"

"Yes, Daddy,' I said, but I never talked to strangers anyway. Only ghosts."

"I ended up on the couch that night, but I slept very little. Miss Sarah's crying kept me up for half the night. After a while, I looked down at Jacob. He was trying to sleep on the floor next to me."

"'Jacob, are you sleeping?"

"He rolled his eyes and said, 'Well, you're looking right at me, Zack. You know damn well I ain't."

"All right then, I was just wondering if we should go up and ask Miss Sarah to be quiet so we can get some sleep."

"Zack, I don't think it's a good idea. You wake Daddy up, and he'll kick the hell out of you."

"I know, but if I was quiet, I could get up there and back without him even knowing."

"What if she screams, Zack? Then what?"

"If she does, I'll cover her mouth real quick."

"You might hurt her, Zack, and I don't think you should hurt her. You heard what Daddy said. She ain't no demon hog. She's a real person. And she's got a baby in her, Zack."

"I don't want to hurt her, but Momma and Daddy, you know what they'll do to her once that baby comes. They're going to kill Miss Sarah, real person or not."

"Jacob sat up next to me and looked straight into my eyes. 'Zack, I don't think you should let them hurt Miss Sarah. She ain't done nothing wrong."

"What can I do? I can't stop Daddy. He's too strong."

"Zack, you do it when he's sleeping. That way, he won't see you coming."

"Are you talking about killing him?"

"Yes, Zack and Momma, too, just like we talked about a while back. You know it needs to be done. They have been hurting you for too long. Now, they want to take Miss Sarah's baby and do the same. It ain't right, Zack. It just ain't right."

"Trust me, Jacob, I'm going to kill both of them. What about Daddy's gun? He keeps it right next to him."

"Well, you're going to have to be quiet and fast. You're going to have to kill Daddy first."

"I don t know, Jacob. What if I get shot?"

"You ain't going to get shot. You just gotta do what I tell you to do."

"I don't know, Jacob. I have to think about this for a while. The only reason I haven't done it is that I can't figure out how to do it without getting myself fucked up in the process."

"If we're gonna do this, we have to do it soon, real soon."

"Well, I'm not doing it tonight, so you can forget that right now."

"Don't have to be tonight, but soon. That's all I'm saying."

"I rolled over and looked up at the ceiling. 'Well, what are we gonna do with Miss Sarah?' I asked."

"Well, once you kill Momma and Daddy, we'll take her into town and give her to the police."

"I couldn't believe what Jacob was saying. I sat up real quick and looked down at him. 'The police? Are you a crazy boy? They're going to lock me up."

"Keep your voice down. You're going to wake Daddy. They won't lock you up. Miss Sarah will tell them you helped her escape. They'll know you weren't the one holding her against her will."

"Well, what if they want to come here and take Momma and Daddy away and find them killed? Then what? And what about the lady hogs down in the freezers?"

"You don't worry about that, Zack. You let me take care of all the other stuff. You just worry about killing Momma and Daddy."

"I was about to argue a little more when Daddy's door flew open upstairs."

"Zack, who the hell are you talking to, you dumb son of a bitch?"

"I yelled back, 'I ain't talking to nobody, Daddy. Just trying to sleep."

"Well, shut your mouth. Between you and this moaning bitch up here, I can't get any sleep myself."

"Daddy slammed his door shut. I looked down at Jacob. He was covering his mouth, trying not to laugh."

"No more talking, boy. You going to get me beat,' I whispered."

"After that, I rolled over, facing the back of the couch."

Sarah knew she was moaning, though it brought some small comfort against the pain. She tried to pry open her eyes but found them swollen and sealed shut as if someone had battered her face with a baseball bat.

Her efforts to move her legs and arms were in vain; they were securely bound to some unknown fixtures. Her tears stung her battered mouth and cheeks. She couldn't help but think about her mother, who must be worrying by now. Sarah envisioned her mother on the phone with her husband, Frank, explaining that Sarah hadn't shown up. She pictured Frank reaching out to the police, becoming a person of interest in his wife's disappearance. Later, her family would go on with their lives, unaware of her gruesome fate at the hands of a deranged family.

Thoughts about the horrors they might inflict upon her raced through her mind. Would they torture her, assault her, or worse? Then, the daunting question of what they'd do with her and her unborn baby's lifeless bodies arose. Would they throw them into a roaring fire, reducing them to unrecognizable ash, or would they drag them into the woods, burying them in a shallow, unmarked grave? There would be no funeral, no flowers, no tearful eulogy. There would never be a gravesite for her husband and family to visit. Instead, she and her baby would gradually be forgotten, their memories fading while the surrounding forest forever imprisoned them.

Sarah attempted to move her legs again, but the bindings held fast, as did her arms. It was apparent she wasn't their first captive. A suffocating sense of hopelessness pervaded her thoughts, yet she understood she had to try, not just for her own survival but for the sake of her baby.

Uncertain of when dawn would break, Sarah recognized that escaping while the house slept might be her best chance. She gritted her teeth in preparation to free her wrists from their restraints, but then she heard a voice. She exhaled softly, her body tense as she attempted to identify its source. The house was silent for a moment, then the voice returned, a whisper from downstairs.

Zack whispered to himself, though she couldn't decipher his words. Nevertheless, it was clear that only one voice spoke. Zack was talking to himself. She turned her head slightly, straining to hear what he was saying. That's when a door down the hallway burst open with violent force. Her heart raced as she feared that someone had heard her efforts to free herself and was now coming to inflict further harm.

Heavy footsteps echoed in her direction before they abruptly halted. It was Charlie. He yelled at Zack to stop talking, punctuating his command with a series of expletives. She expected Charlie to enter the room and harm her in retaliation, but he didn't. Instead, he retreated down the hallway, slamming his bedroom door behind him, and all was quiet once more.

Sarah remained still for several minutes, listening intently for any signs of movement before she cautiously resumed her struggle to break free. Her baby kicked, reminding her that she couldn't let them harm her child. Sarah persevered, gnawing at her restraints with raw and bleeding wrists through most of the night. By morning, she was nearly free.

Sarah knew she was on the brink of escape, even if it meant navigating her way to freedom while virtually blind. Somehow, she'd find her way back to the road for help. She was so close now; the ropes had slackened enough for her to use her fingers to untie the knot.

A bump from under the bed rocked the mattress. Sarah froze, thinking perhaps she had rocked the rickety bed. But as she lay motionless, the bed gently rocked. Someone or something was lying below her, separated only by a single mattress.

Sarah held her breath, her heart pounding in her chest. Whatever was under the bed exhaled, a long gurgling breath followed by a bubbling cough.

Sarah whispered, "Hello, is someone there?"

Another deep gurgling breath rattled from under the bed, followed by a hissing voice.

"Hurry, they will kill you."

Sarah's lips trembled, overcome with fear too great to respond.

The voice hissed, "Hurry."

With renewed determination, Sarah struggled to free herself from the confines of her bed. Each movement was agonizing, the weight of fear pressing down on her like a suffocating blanket. But as she slid her hand free, she heard another sound—a faint rustling beside her. Something was disturbing the air beside her, and a faint whiff of soap wafted her way.

"Whose there?" she asked cautiously.

Darleen's fist smashed into her nose. Sarah heard and felt the awful crunch of shattered bone, followed by blood pouring down both sides of her face. Sarah gasped in pain as Darleen delivered another blow. Her front teeth shattered, sending broken fragments to the back of her throat. In desperation, Sarah turned her head to avoid another blow.

For a moment, the beating ceased. Darleen was breathing heavily before she delivered a final merciless blow to the side of Sarah's head. All was black. There was no pain.

"I must have nodded pretty quickly because the next thing I knew, I woke up to Momma slapping me in the face."

"Get up, boy. Get up off my couch, you filthy shit."

"I got up quick, covering my head. 'Sorry, Momma. I'm sorry."

"You're going to be. Never let me catch you sleeping in like some lazy dog. You've got work to do. I need you to run into town and pick up some rubbing alcohol."

"I was so excited about going into town that I didn't bother asking what she needed the alcohol for. I didn't care much, either. Momma and Daddy hardly ever let me go into town."

"Momma pulled a handful of money from her apron and looked me in the eyes. 'Now you listen, and you listen good. Once you get into town, don't you say anything about Miss Sarah. Do you understand me? Someone finds out about her, and we're all fucked. Don't talk to anyone. Just pick up the alcohol and hightail it straight back home.' Momma kissed the top of my head. 'Now you go on and get. I have to tend to Miss Sarah."

"I grabbed the keys off the hook by the door and left."

"I know I shouldn't have, but I always enjoyed it when I go to town. Even if people looked at me kind of strangely, it felt good to be away from the house for a bit."

"Eventually, I bought the rubbing alcohol at the only market in town. A pretty girl was working at the counter. I could tell she wasn't a lady hog. She was just a normal young girl about my age. I wished Momma and Daddy hadn't messed my face up so badly. That way, maybe I could've got a girl like her for my own, but I could tell she was a little scared of me. So I just took my change from her and left so she didn't have to look at me anymore."

"When I got in the truck, Jacob looked over at me. He knew I was upset."

It's okay, Zack. It ain't your fault you look the way you do. You are a good boy deep inside, and that's what matters."

"I looked at Jacob. He was always saying nice things like that."

"Well, that may be true, but I think you are the only one who knows it. I was a little teary-eyed, so I looked away from him before starting the truck and heading home."

"I was about halfway home when I saw a state trooper parked on the side of the highway. It looked like he was talking on his radio."

"Don't see them around here very much,' I said to Jacob."

"Probably nothing. Don't worry about yourself none,' Jacob said."

"Well, we got about half a mile further up the road, and damn if there wasn't another trooper. He was outside his cruiser, looking down off the side of the road like he was searching for something."

"We better get home, Zach. I have a feeling they are looking for Miss Sarah,' said Jacob."

"I laid the pedal down, then Jacob yelled, 'Now, Zack, slow down before you get yourself stopped."

"Okay, 'I'm just a little scared, that's all."

"It's going to be okay, Zack. Just stay calm."

"Just as he finished saying that, we rounded a curve, and off the right shoulder were two sheriff trucks parked on the side of the roadway. Both deputies were outside their trucks, doing the same thing as the trooper. They were walking up the road, looking down the hill. I knew then they were looking for Miss Sarah. I could feel my heart pounding in my chest. Jacob knew I was frightened."

"Just calm down now. We're almost home. Just take her real easy."

"Jacob, I can't calm down. What if they find out we have Miss Sarah up in my room?"

"They aren't going to."

"Well, what if they do? They'll lock me up forever."

"Not if you help her, Zack. Remember what I said. If you help her get away from Momma and Daddy, they might let you go. You have done nothing wrong."

"I'm scared, Jacob."

"Zack, you just calm down and listen. We'll take it one step at a time, starting with getting Miss Sarah out of the house and away from Momma and Daddy."

"I thought we were going to kill them?"

"One step at a time. We still have time to plan."

"We drove around the last curve before my driveway, and on the left side of the road about where Miss Sarah had parked her car was another state trooper. He was walking toward my driveway, looking down at the road. I guess he heard us coming because he looked up and waved his hand for me to stop. I turned into my driveway and waited for him to get to the truck."

"When he got to my door, I forgot to roll down my window, so he started knocking on it. I froze for a minute. I was afraid to look him in the face. I looked at Jacob. I could tell he was frightened too, but I did what he told me and rolled down the window."

"The trooper kind of looked at me funny before asking, 'You live around here, son?'"

"Yes, sir."

"Whereabouts?"

"I pointed up toward where my house was. 'Right up there, sir.'"

"He glanced up at my road. 'What's your name, son?'"

"Zackary Charles Williams."

"You got an ID on you?"

"No, sir."

"Why not? You know you can't be driving without a driver's license."

"I said the first thing that came to mind. 'Sir, I just forgot it at home.' I didn't have a license."

"Where are you coming from, boy?"

"I had to run into town for my Momma. She needed some rubbing alcohol."

"He scratched his head and said, 'Well, I'll tell you something. I'm out here because I'm looking for a young woman who has gone missing. Some folks saw her car parked right about here yesterday. They said it looked like the car had a flat tire. Have you seen that car around here?'"

"I could feel my heart race. 'No, sir, I haven't seen any cars parked around here.'"

"No? Well, how about a woman, about 5'6" woman with long brown hair, possibly pregnant, in a white tank top and blue shorts? Her name is Sarah Buchanan."

"No, sir, I haven't seen any women either."

"The trooper glanced up toward my road again and asked,

"How far back do you say your house is?"

"I started getting scared then, but Jacob whispered, 'Be calm, Zack. Just answer the question."

"Well, sir, I didn't say how far, but if you're wondering, I'd say maybe half a mile or so, give or take a bit."

"He looked up at my road again. 'Road looks a little rough. Do you think I could get my cruiser up there, maybe have a look around?"

"Oh no, sir, the road gets worse a little farther. I got to go all the way up there in four-wheel drive."

"The trooper nodded his head. 'All right then, go on and get home, but do me a favor. Call us if you see Miss Buchanan or her car, and make sure you have your license with you next time you're driving out and about."

"Okay, officer, I'll call if I see her, and I won't ever drive without my license again, I promise."

"He smiled nice at me and said, 'All right then, have a nice day, son. Oh, one last thing before you go. Let your parents know the law may be up your way to look around.' He tipped his hat and walked back to his cruiser."

"I'll tell you, I was so glad that was over. I started up our road, shaking like a dog passing peach pits. I looked over at Jacob. He was bouncing around on account of all the ruts. I said, 'Goddamn, that was close."

"You did good, Zack, except we may have a problem. Did you catch what he said about the law coming around to have a look?"

"I heard him, but if you are so hell-bent on setting Miss Sarah loose, why didn't you want me to tell him about Miss Sarah?"

"Because, Zack, we got to deal with Momma and Daddy first, and we got to make sure Miss Sarah's on our side and won't say we were part of keeping her."

"Jacob was always thinking.

"All right then. Should I tell Momma and Daddy about the trooper?"

"No, Zack, don't tell them anything. We don't want them to get scared and throw Miss Sarah in the pig pond."

"Okay, you're right. Daddy would do that, especially if he thought the law was coming."

"Damn right, he would."

"A few minutes later, we pulled up to the front of the house. Daddy came out the front door looking really mad. I got out of the truck with Momma's things. Before he could say anything, I said, 'Sorry it took so long, Daddy. There was an accident down the road a bit."

"That didn't seem to calm him down a bit. 'Shut your damn mouth and get in the house. I don't want to hear your fucking lies. You know your Momma needs her things."

"When I walked past Daddy, he kicked my ass so damn hard I damn near fell. I didn't even look back, though. I was so used to that bullshit that it didn't bother me much anymore."

"When I got in the house, Momma stood in the kitchen, and she looked pissed."

"Where in the hell have you been? Your daddy and I got work to do, and you are messing around like you are the only thing that matters around here."

"I could tell by the expression on Momma's face she was about to light into me."

"No, Momma, I wasn't messing around. There was an accident a ways down the road. I couldn't help it."

"Before I knew what was happening, Momma hit me as hard as she could across my mouth."

"I don't want to hear any more from you, boy.' Momma grabbed the rubbing alcohol from me and walked out of the room, hollering for Daddy to get the bowl from the sink."

"Daddy slapped the back of my head as he walked past me and said, 'Come upstairs, boy. Your Momma might need some help."

"Daddy got the bowl, and I followed him upstairs to my room."

"When we got up there, poor Miss Sarah looked terrible. Her swollen eyes were closed, and her lips were all busted up. She was lying there, crying and trying to say something. That was the first time I ever felt bad for someone while they were suffering."

Sarah's eyelids fluttered open, her vision blurred by tears and pain. Through the haze, she could discern the nightmarish figures of the Williams family looming over her. Darleen's silhouette was distorted, her features twisted into a grotesque mask as she brandished what looked like a knife in one hand and a roll of bandages in the other. Charlie stood beside her, clutching a large metal bowl with an unsettling determination.

As the reality of her situation sank in, Sarah's heart plummeted. She knew, with a sickening certainty, that this was the end. They were going to cut her baby out of her, and she would bleed to death before their eyes.

Desperation clawed at her throat as she tried to plead with them, to beg for mercy in the face of their madness. But her words were choked off by the fear that gripped her, leaving her voice nothing more than a feeble whisper.

"Please, Darleen, please don't hurt my baby." Sarah could hear the garbled sounds coming from her shattered mouth and knew Darleen couldn't understand her, and neither would she care.

Darleen acted as if she hadn't heard anything. She roughly untied Sarha's left leg. "Daddy, you hold the back of her leg and don't let her wiggle around. It's going to be a big fucking mess here in a second, and I don't need it to get worse with her kicking."

Sarah's heart pounded in her chest as Charlie's hands, rough and unyielding, closed around her shin like a vice, trapping her in place. She felt the cold sweat break out on her skin as Darleen slid the metal bowl onto the bed, its presence casting a sinister shadow over the room.

With trembling limbs, Sarah watched in horror as Darleen's movements became deliberate and methodical. The glint of the knife against her Achilles tendon sent a shiver down her spine, the metal blade poised to cut through flesh and sinew with ruthless precision.

Time seemed to slow to a crawl as Sarah braced herself for the inevitable, the fear twisting in her gut like a coiled serpent ready to strike. She wanted to scream, to beg for mercy, but her shattered mouth couldn't form the words; instead, she whimpered like a child.

"What are you going to do?" asked Zack.

"I'm gonna cut the back of her ankles real deep so she can't run out on us. See, I went in here this morning, and I could tell she had been trying to get herself loose, had one of her hands almost completely untied." Darleen smiled at Sarah. "Isn't that right, baby doll?"

Sarah squirmed, whimpering in fear.

"Shut your fucking mouth, girl. I'm tired of you and your bullshit," Darleen yelled as she ran the knife fiercely across the back of Sarah's ankle.

With a sickening snap, Sarah's Achilles tendon gave way beneath the pressure of Darleen's blade, recoiling like a rubber band into her leg. Agony tore through her body like wildfire, igniting every nerve ending with searing pain. She couldn't contain the scream that tore from her throat, a primal cry of torment and despair that echoed through the room.

But her cries were met with only cold indifference from the Williams family, their faces twisted into grotesque masks of madness and malice.

There was no mercy in their eyes, no flicker of remorse for the suffering they had inflicted.

As Sarah writhed in agony, the realization dawned on her with chilling clarity—she was at the mercy of monsters, and there would be no escape from their clutches.

"I didn't know what to do. I looked at my closet, and Jacob was just standing there. He didn't know what to do either. All we could do was watch. Finally, Momma took one of Daddy's butchering knives, cutting Miss Sarah right on the backside of her ankle. Miss Sarah screamed out and tried kicking her leg free, but it wasn't much use. Once Daddy gets hold of something, he doesn't let go till the job is done. So then Momma cut the other one, crippling Miss Sarah real good."

"Poor Miss Sarah was screaming, as I had never heard a person scream before. She started thrashing around so badly, I thought she would bloody up my bed, something awful. She didn't though. Momma and Daddy held on to her tight. A few minutes later, Miss Sarah stopped her thrashing around. She let out one last scream, then just kinda went limp for a bit."

"That's when Momma poured alcohol on one of her cleaning rags and started cleaning up Miss Sarah's legs. Momma had skills that way. She cleaned and bandaged her ankles up really nice. Then she smiled at Miss Sarah and said, 'Didn't want to do that, girl, but it was for the best. Now, we don't have to worry about you running off with that baby. It also means we won't have to keep your legs all tied up. Your arms are a different story, though. We'll have to keep them tied up until we can trust one another."

"Miss Sarah said nothing. She just lay there, crying and moaning. Her body was quivering all over."

"Momma, is she going to be all right? She looks like she's hurting real bad."

"Oh, she'll be fine. We need to leave her be for a bit and give her time to collect herself some."

"Daddy, real careful like, handed me the bowl and said, 'Run this down to the cellar and clean it up."

"It was about overflowing with Miss Sarah's blood, so I had to be careful going down the stairs. I knew damn well what Momma would do if I spilled one drop on the floor."

"I had a hell of a time sleeping that night. That goddamn couch was as hard as a fucking rock. Plus, Jacob had a terrible snoring problem. And worst of all was Momma and Daddy's bed squeaking on and on as they were making all kinds of grunting noises. It sounded like a bunch of hogs fucking up in there. I hated that shit when they would get at it."

"Luckily, things finally quieted down after a bit. I could hear Miss Sarah crying in my room and one of Momma's old clocks ticking. It didn't take long before I fell asleep."

"I woke up before the light. I couldn't get that girl from the store off my mind. She was so damn pretty. I knew she wouldn't have anything to do with the likes of me, but I got to thinking maybe I could take her. Maybe I could kill her. I know this sounds crazy, but sometimes I helped Daddy kill one of them lady hogs, and I felt, well, like we had a connection for a minute, like the killing was special between us, like we shared something really pretty. Doctor, during those times, right before their eyes went dead. I liked to watch their souls float away. I have to admit there were times I almost started crying. It was that special to me. Especially if I was holding their face real close to mine so I could feel their last breath, I know they were nothing but hogs, but goddamn, some of them were really pretty. Kinda like that girl."

"Anyway, I knew I was going to do it. I was going to get ahold of her, and I was going to share that with her. I was going to be the last thing she ever saw."

"Jacob must have felt me stirring around 'cause he sat up next to me, rubbing his eyes, and said, 'Zack, what are you doing awake?"

"I knew better than to tell him what I was thinking about, so I just said, 'Don't you worry about it. I just can't sleep."

"Jacob looked me square in the eyes and smiled like he knew what I was thinking. 'Zack, I hope you ain't thinking about that girl in town. If you are, just forget it. She was afraid of you. If you go sniffing around that store, she might call the cops."

"Well, goddamn, you think you are so fucking smart, but you're not. I wasn't thinking about anything but knocking you in the head. Another thing, I have plans for tomorrow, and I would appreciate a little privacy for once."

"Well, if you want some privacy, that's fine with me. But if you get yourself in trouble, I ain't gonna be there to get you out.' Then he lay back down and pretended to go to sleep."

"I felt terrible. I'd never talked to Jacob like that before. But goddamn it, I couldn't have him tailing along all the time trying to tell me what was right and wrong. Sometimes a man's got to handle his shit. I didn't say anything more to him that night. I just kind of laid there and waited for the light. In the morning, I was going to ask Daddy if I could use his truck and go back into town."

"I woke up to Momma again slapping the shit out of me. She was yelling, 'Goddamn you, you lazy fucking dog. I told you not to sleep in."

"I shot right up off that couch and said, 'Momma, I'm sorry. I just couldn't sleep last night. All that noise up there kept me awake."

"Momma's eyes opened up real wide like they did when she was pissed, and she said, 'What the fuck are you talking about, boy? Are you talking about the racket your daddy and I were making? Were you listening in like some kind of sick-ass horny toad?"

"I was terrified then. I knew she was thinking way off the mark, so I said, 'No, Momma, I was talking about Miss Sarah up there. She was crying all night.' "Momma pointed at me and said, 'Boy, you better never let me catch you acting like a horny toad, you hear me? Don't you ever talk about what me and your daddy do in our bedroom. Do you understand me?"

"Now I knew damn well Momma was talking crazy shit, so I just said, 'Momma, you ain't never gonna catch me being a horny toad, and I promise you ain't never gonna hear me talk about what you and Daddy do up in your room."

"Momma kind of straightened up and smiled. 'Well then, now that's settled, why don't you wash up while I get some breakfast started?"

"I walked around the couch and hugged Momma, then went to the cellar and cleaned up. Before long, I could smell Momma cooking bacon and eggs."

"When I came back up the stairs and into the kitchen, Daddy was already sitting at the table. He was sipping a cup of coffee and pretending to read the same newspaper he had for over a month. I don't know why the fuck he did that. We all knew damn well he couldn't read. I guess he felt like he was some sort of smart guy or something. Anyway, he looked up at me, then went back to running his finger across the sentences."

"What have you got planned today?' Daddy asked me.

"I thought maybe this was my chance to ask about using the truck, but damn, I wasn't sure how to do it, so I just said, 'Well, Daddy, I was thinking if Momma has anything she needs picked up in town, I'd go get it for her."

"Daddy looked up from his paper. I could tell by his squinting eyes he wasn't sure what to make of what I just said. 'Now, why the hell would I let you go running around town for Momma? You know damn well I don't like you driving around. The only reason I let you do it yesterday was that your Momma needed my help with Miss Sarah, and by the way, you fucked that up by coming home late and making up some bullshit excuses."

"Well, Daddy, what I told you was the truth. I wouldn't have taken any chances of screwing that up. Yesterday, I did good. I just thought if it were okay, I'd give her another try."

"Daddy looked over his shoulder at Momma. She turned around from her frying pans. She was listening to us talk."

"Well, Momma, what do you think? You got anything you want Zack to pick up for you in town?"

"Momma looked at me. 'Zack, there are a few things I need, but you don't go fucking things up. It seems like you can't go through a single day without fucking up. I love you, but you are about dumb as a rock. I won't stand for you getting into any more trouble."

"I knew things were looking pretty good, so I said, 'Momma, I promise there ain't going to be no hassles. I'll go into town, get your things, and drive straight home."

"Momma put her hand on Daddy's shoulder. He looked up at her and smiled. 'Well, we got a few things to do around here. I guess you can run into town and help your Momma."

"I damn near jumped right out of my chair. I was so damn happy."

"Thank you, Daddy. Thank you, Momma. I promise I won't get into any trouble. I'll go to town and come straight back home."

"Momma and Daddy both smiled at me before Momma went back to her cooking. Then she said, 'Daddy, we got us a real sweet boy, don't we?"

"Daddy winked at me and said, 'Yes, Momma, we do. We got ourselves a real sweet, stupid boy."

"Daddy smiled at me the nicest he had in a long time, then he looked down at that damn paper and started running his finger across it like he was reading again."

Sarah awoke in sheer agony. Her ankles throbbed in cruel harmony with her racing heart. The injuries to her ankles had grown dire, and a nauseating heat of infection radiated up her calves. Attempting to pry open her eyes, she was met with unyielding resistance. Shrouded in an unsettling darkness, the room offered no solace or means of escape.

She strained against the ropes, binding her arms with a renewed sense of desperation. This time, however, Darleen or Charlie had cruelly tightened the knots beyond any hope of freedom. Her fingers and hands had become numb, alien appendages that refused to obey her will.

Sarah battled the urge to scream, acutely aware that such outbursts would incur further harm from Darleen. She couldn't bear another brutal beating like the one she had endured the previous night.

Struggling to hold back her tears, she soon succumbed to their relentless flow, her silent sobs betraying the depth of her despair.

For unknown reasons beyond rationality, these twisted fucks were going to kill her and her baby. She changed tactics. There would be no more physical altercations with them. That had proven to be a painful failure. There was no way to overpower a group of lunatics. She decided her best chance of self-preservation and eventual escape would be to do whatever they said.

From below, muffled voices of the family drifted up the staircase. They had awoken, engaged in some conversation she couldn't decipher, but all three were part of it. She couldn't help but imagine the kind of witless, inane chatter that might be transpiring downstairs. The absurdity of it all felt like it could push her to the brink of hysterical laughter.

A curious scent, reminiscent of cooking bacon, wafted through the air, tingling her senses. However, something about the aroma set off alarms in her mind, a primordial warning that whatever was cooking was not that of beast or plant.

Sarah shivered uncontrollably as the sickening scent of human flesh permeated the air around her, adding yet another vile layer of repulsion that seemed to encompass the twisted family.

Sarah lay there, her nerves taut, waiting for Darleen's inevitable return with *breakfast*.

A while later, the distant echoes of yelling downstairs, followed by a heavy thud, reached her ears. It was clear that someone was being subjected to a beating, and it sounded like Zack was the unfortunate recipient. While she couldn't make out the words exchanged, Zack's fearful voice was unmistakable. For a brief moment, she felt a pang of sympathy for the boy, but it evaporated as quickly as it appeared.

A harsh slap soon accompanied the sound of a slammed screen door. Darleen uttered something, and Zack responded.

Sarah found herself wishing for the chance to repay the cruelty they had shown her. She'd relish each strike, take her time with each of them, and delight in the pain etched across their faces.

She reluctantly pulled herself from this vengeful reverie, aware she was teetering on the precipice of insanity. While she listened to the steady thumping, resembling wood being chopped outside, she couldn't help but feel entrapped by the sounds and smells of this deranged household.

Engrossed in the rhythmic thumping, she hardly noticed when the water ceased running and the clattering dishes in the kitchen stopped. The only sound that remained was the subtle creak of the stairs, making its presence known as someone ascended.

Darleen was coming. Sarah listened in horror as the thumping outside merged with the stairs creaking—creak, thump, creak, thump, creak, creak, thump, creak, thump. Finally, the creaking stopped, but the thumping maintained its cadence.

A gurgling whisper emerged from the depths beneath the bed, sending shivers down Sarah's spine. "They're going to kill you," it hissed, the words dripping with a malevolent urgency that chilled her to the bone.

Sarah's heart raced as the reality of her situation crashed down upon her with crushing force. She was trapped between the merciless intentions of the Williams family and the ominous warning from the unseen presence below.

The bedroom door creaked open, and Darleen slinked into the room. Sarah had to suppress an overpowering urge to scream.

"Well, baby doll, how are you feeling, hon?" Darleen inquired with a false sweetness that sent shivers down Sarah's spine.

Sarah remained silent as Darleen gently placed a plate of bacon and eggs on the nightstand next to the bed. She sat beside Sarah, her clammy palm touching Sarah's feverish forehead.

Sarah cringed as Darleen's cold, revolting hand made contact. She was outraged that this vile woman dared to lay hands on her. While Sarah harbored a burning desire to end Darleen's life, she concealed her emotions. Her chance for vengeance would come. Sarah was sure of that.

Darleen's brows furrowed with concern. "Oh, baby, you got yourself a bit of a fever. We're going to have to get some food in you." Darleen smiled, "I told you, honey, I'm going to take good care of you and that baby."

Darleen picked up the plate and offered a piece of smoked flesh to Sarah's lips. Even though she had intended to comply with their wishes, there was no way she would consume the detestable concoction.

With sheer determination, Sarah gritted her teeth, clamping her mouth shut despite the agony coursing through her body.

Darleen's frustration boiled over, her grip tightening as she pressed the meat forcefully against Sarah's swollen lips.

"Listen to me, damn it," she spat, her voice seething with anger. "If you don't eat, you're gonna hurt that baby, and I ain't gonna let you hurt that baby."

Sarah's defiance sparked Darleen's fury to new heights. With a growl of rage, Darleen seized Sarah's face in a vice-like grip, her fingers digging into Sarah's flesh as she attempted to force the meat into her mouth.

But Sarah refused to yield; her jaw clenched with unyielding determination as she turned away, denying Darleen's relentless assault. Enraged by Sarah's resistance, Darleen's desperation reached a fever pitch.

In a desperate bid to overpower Sarah, Darleen pried her lips apart and attempted to insert her fingers into her mouth. With a surge of adrenaline, Sarah summoned every ounce of strength within her and clamped down with ferocious resolve.

A sickening snap echoed through the room as Sarah's jaws closed around Darleen's fingers, the taste of blood and flesh flooding her mouth. Despite the pain shooting through her own body, Sarah felt a grim satisfaction wash over her as she heard the unmistakable sound of bones breaking beneath the pressure of her bite.

Darleen's screams pierced the air, a symphony of agony and rage as she fought to free her fingers from Sarah's relentless grip. But Sarah's resolve remained unbroken, her jaws locked tight around Darleen's wounded hand.

In a desperate bid to escape, Darleen clawed frantically at Sarah's face, her nails seeking out her eyes with savage intent. Sarah's cries of pain mingled with the sounds of tearing flesh as Darleen's nails pried open her swollen eyes, threatening to gouge them from their sockets.

The agony was unbearable, a relentless assault on Sarah's senses as she writhed in torment. With no other choice, she opened her mouth, releasing a guttural scream of pain and desperation.

As Darleen fell backward off the bed, her fingers freed from the savage vice of Sarah's shattered mouth, a surge of primal rage engulfed her. Blood dripped from her mangled hand, staining the floor crimson as she staggered to her feet, her eyes ablaze with fury.

Sarah lay trembling on the bed, tears mingling with Darleen's blood as she stared up at her assailant, her heart pounding in her chest.

Darleen's twisted visage loomed over her, a grotesque mask of pain and hatred that sent a chill down her spine.

"Baby doll, you fucked up real bad. I'm going to do something so awful to you; you're gonna wanna die before I'm through."

Darleen stumbled out of the room, her wounded hand throbbing with each heartbeat. She made her way to the kitchen, her steps unsteady as she reached the sink. With trembling hands, she turned on the faucet and let the cool water cascade over her injured fingers, washing away the blood that stained her skin.

The pain was excruciating, a constant reminder of the brutality she had endured at Sarah's hands. Her fingers were mangled, the bones shattered by the force of Sarah's jaws. They would never be the same again, forever scarred by the encounter with that vile woman.

Wrapping her injured hand in a towel, Darleen sank into a chair at the kitchen table. Anger simmering inside her, a boiling cauldron of hatred and vengeance. She was going to make Sarah pay for what she had done, to inflict as much pain as possible without crossing the line into murder, not yet.

As she rocked back and forth in her chair, Darleen's mind raced with thoughts of retribution. How could she make Sarah suffer as she had suffered? And then, like a bolt of lightning striking from the darkness, the answer came to her.

Sarah's tears flowed unchecked, a silent testament to her pain and despair. Every inch of her body throbbed with agony, each injury a cruel reminder of the horrors she had endured. The scratches on her eyes burned with searing pain, her ankles throbbed with the heat of infection, and her hands throbbed from lack of circulation, the remnants of her struggle against her captors.

As she lay there, bound and broken, the realization of her grim fate settled upon her like a heavy shroud. Trapped in this decrepit house, at the mercy of psychotic cannibals, Sarah knew that her chances of survival were slim at best. The thought of dying alone and forgotten in this forsaken place filled her with a bone-deep dread.

But even in the face of such despair, Sarah refused to surrender to hopelessness. With every fiber of her being, she clung to the flickering flame of defiance, determined not to give her captors the satisfaction of killing her. Instead, she would end her life on her terms.

Sarah's desperate attempt to end her suffering took a harrowing turn as she struggled to hold her breath, willing herself to succumb to the darkness. With every passing moment, her lungs screamed for air, her body convulsing with the effort to deny itself the life-giving oxygen it so desperately craved.

But just as Sarah teetered on the brink of unconsciousness, a sudden sensation jolted her back to reality. A gentle thump emanated from the depths of her womb, a small but unmistakable movement that filled her with a surge of unexpected emotion. Her baby was alive, a tiny beacon of hope amidst the darkness that threatened to consume her.

Tears welled in Sarah's eyes as she felt the fluttering of life within her, a bittersweet reminder of the precious gift she carried despite the horrors that surrounded her. In that fleeting moment, she found the strength to continue fighting, clinging to the fragile hope that bound her to her unborn child.

With renewed determination, Sarah vowed to protect her baby at all costs, to endure whatever suffering lay ahead if only to ensure their survival. In the midst of her darkest hour, the tiny flutter of life within her womb became her reason to keep fighting.

"Daddy and I chopped a whole mess of wood that day, punishment for something stupid I'd said. I was so goddamn worn out I just about dropped when he said we were all done. We must have cut three or four cords. I sat down and wiped the sweat off my face with my shirt. It was getting late in the afternoon. The sun was just setting, but it was still damn hot."

"Daddy sat down beside me and patted my back. 'You did all right today, boy. Do you still feel up to running into town for Momma?'"

"I looked at Daddy. 'Well, hell yeah, I still feel up to it, Daddy. I hardly ever get out.'"

"Daddy smiled at me and said, 'Well then, let's go on and see what your momma's got in mind for you.'"

"We walked back to the house. It was only about fifty yards from where we did our chopping. I remember that day so clearly. I remember looking around that yard and feeling pretty good about things. This was my home, and this was my family. I knew we weren't perfect, but shit, I guess things could be a lot worse."

"We walked into the house and into the kitchen. Momma was sitting at the kitchen table, looking like shit. Her face was covered in sweat, and her entire body was shaking. She held her left hand over a bowl, sewing up two fingers with her right. She was bleeding pretty severely. She looked up at Daddy and me and smiled."

"Well, boys, I'll bet you're wondering why the fuck I'm sewing up these fingers. That little pain-in-the-ass bitch upstairs decided she would not eat her breakfast, so I tried persuading her a bit. That's when she damn near bit my hand off."

"Momma held up her shaking right hand so we could have a better look. Blood was running down her fingers and dripping into that bowl."

"Daddy walked up to Momma and put his arm around her. 'Momma, do you want us to take care of her? We'll be careful and cut that baby clean out. Then we'll chop that bitch to pieces."

"No, Daddy, I'm gonna take care of her myself. We ain't cutting no baby out of her. I ain't taking no chances and hurting it. Besides, you might be good at butchering, but it's a whole different thing when it comes to birthing a baby."

"I felt pretty bad for Momma, but I knew how damn mean she could be. So I figured Momma probably had it coming."

"Daddy and I sat at the table and watched Momma finish her stitching. By the time she was finished, her fingers were swollen, but she held them up and could bend them a little. She poured some rubbing alcohol on her hand and wiped all the blood away. They didn't look so bad then. She asked Daddy to wrap her fingers with some gauze. It was too hard for her to do that with one hand."

"Daddy was gentle with Momma. He wasn't as good as Momma when it came to patching a wound, but he got the job done. Momma smiled at Daddy when he finished up."

"Daddy, you did real good,' she said."

"Daddy smiled back at her, then took the bowl into the sink. While he was washing it, he said, 'Momma, do you still need Zack to run into town?'"

"Momma looked at me. 'I guess so. I'm gonna need some more rubbing alcohol and bandages before the night is through.'"

"I was so damn happy she hadn't changed her mind."

"Momma stood up and walked over to the drawer where she kept her money. She took a pad of paper and some bills from it and sat beside me. She looked at me real nice and said, 'Now listen, boy. I'm gonna make you a list of things I need you to get. Get everything on it, okay, baby? Don't fuck things up and forget something.'"

"I won't, Momma."

"Momma started scribbling some things down on that piece of paper while telling me what she needed in town. She couldn't read or write either. So she said, 'First off, I'm going to need four bottles of rubbing alcohol. Then I'm going to need about four rolls of gauze and a pack of Band-Aids, not the small ones; I need those big ones.'"

"Momma looked up from her scribbling and smiled. 'Do you think you can remember all that, boy?'"

"I stood up, took the money and paper, and put it in my front pocket. 'I won't forget nothing, Momma. I'm just going downstairs real quick and cleaning up, then I'll head out.'"

"Momma smiled and held her arms up so I would hug her. I did it, then headed downstairs. I wasn't all that concerned with cleaning up. What I wanted was Daddy's big knife. I was hoping before the night was through that me and the pretty girl in the store and I could still spend some time together."

"I was careful not to make too much noise. I knew Momma and Daddy would never let me go anywhere again if they knew I was sneaking out with Daddy's knife. She was there when I opened the toolbox. I had to be gentle when I put her down the back of my pants. Daddy kept that damn thing so damn sharp I bet you could split a hair with it."

"I washed my hands and face in the sink, then headed back up the stairs. I should have been louder; when I walked into the kitchen, Daddy was standing behind Momma with his hand down her shirt. So I turned around quick and went back down the stairs. Thank God they didn't see me. Otherwise, they would have beat the shit out of me for spying or something."

"I waited a few minutes, then walked back up the stairs real loud, and I started whistling. When I got up into the kitchen, Momma looked a little flushed, but at least Daddy didn't have his hands down her shirt. They were just standing there by the stove, smiling at me. I didn't know what to do, so I just took the keys off the table and said, 'I'll be back soon.'"

"Momma said, 'Okay, boy, just be careful.'"

"Before I was out of the room, I saw Daddy out of the corner of my eye throwing that hand back down Momma's shirt. I don't know what the fuck got into those two, but damn, I was glad to be out of there for a bit. What kind of kid wants to see that shit?"

"When I got outside, it was already dark, but it was one of those warm summer nights. I always liked that time of year. I opened the truck door, and who the hell did I see? None other than Jacob sitting in the passenger seat. He crossed his arms and looked straight ahead like he was all pissed off."

"Oh hell no, boy. I already told you you ain't going with me. Now you go on and get out."

"Jacob didn't say anything. He just sat there, looking straight ahead. I was getting a little frustrated with him."

"You hear me, boy? You're not going anywhere with me tonight. Now get the fuck out of this truck before I kick the shit out of you."

"I felt bad for talking that way, but dammit, I didn't want him around. He looked at me, and I could see he was crying."

"Then he said, 'I'll get out, Zack, but you know you'll get yourself in trouble. You're all I got, and I can't stand thinking about you getting hurt."

"That goddamn boy always knew how to get to me. But, like I said, I needed some privacy for once. So I said, 'Jacob, please let me alone just this once. I'll come home to you, and we will never be apart again. I just need some privacy tonight."

"Jacob looked at me really sad and then slid across the seat toward me. Then he jumped out of the truck and walked around toward the back of the house."

"I was half tempted not to go, but I wanted to give that girl in town something special. So I hopped in, fired that old truck up, and headed toward town. That old Marshall Tucker song started playing on the radio. I turned her up and rolled down the window. I knew this night would be the best night I ever had."

Brush With the Devil

"It was around 9:45 p.m. and damn near closing time when I got to the store. I walked in, and sure as shit, there she was, standing at the cash register reading a magazine, twirling her hair, and chewing gum like some kinda kid. She didn't even look at me when I walked in. I picked up one of the little red baskets they had and gathered up Momma's things. No one else was in the store, so I didn't feel all awkward with people looking at me. I took my time. I noticed a sign outside the door saying the store closed at ten. That was good. It was already nine-thirty, and I didn't want to wait too long for her to lock up and head home."

"After a bit, I walked up to the register. She looked up at me with the prettiest eyes I'd ever seen."

Kimberly Wilson's fingers tightened around the edges of her magazine, the glossy pages offering little solace against the unsettling presence of the boy from the previous day. His eyes, devoid of life, seemed to pierce through her like icy daggers, sending shivers down her spine.

Forcing a strained smile, Kimberly attempted to break the tension. "How are you tonight, sir?" she ventured, her voice trembling as she awaited his response.

"Okay, I guess, just running around getting things for my Momma is all," Zackary replied, his words barely audible over the hum of the fluorescent lights.

Kimberly nodded, her smile faltering as she returned to her magazine, her mind racing with unease. Despite her attempts to appear nonchalant, she couldn't shake the feeling of being watched, the weight of Zackary's gaze bearing down on her like a leaden cloak.

Kimberly glanced up at the mirror positioned near the ceiling. Her heart skipped a beat as she caught sight of Zackary's reflection. He moved through the aisles with an eerie calmness, his shopping basket swinging lightly at his side. But each time he neared the cash register, his grin widened into a sinister curve, sending a chill down Kimberly's spine.

The realization dawned on her like a sudden gust of wind – there was something evil lurking behind that innocent facade. With each passing moment, Kimberly's unease grew, a gnawing fear clawing at the edges of her mind as she struggled to comprehend the true nature of Zackary's intentions.

Zackary finally finished picking up a few items before placing his basket on the counter, his dead eyes staring at Kimberly while an evil grin etched his lips.

Zackary whispered, "I got all my Momma's things."

Kimberly hastily scanned the items on the counter, feeling the need to expedite the encounter. She cleared her throat and responded, "Well, that is sweet of you."

"My Momma says I'm a sweet boy; she says that a lot."

Kimberly continued scanning Zackary's items briskly, suspecting he might be mentally disabled, deranged, or a combination of both. The sooner he left the store, the better. She raised her gaze to find him still staring at her with his unnerving, lifeless eyes.

"Well, sir, that will be $14.75."

Kimberly watched Zackary as he reached into his front pocket, fearing he might produce a weapon. Instead, he retrieved a crumpled twenty-dollar bill and placed it on the counter. Kimberly couldn't help but notice Zackary's excessively long and dirty fingernails. She swiftly accepted the bill and returned his change. She was eager to get him out of the store.

"Well, sir, if that is all, I have to close up now."

Zackary didn't utter a word; he merely took his bag and headed for the door, his footsteps echoing ominously against the tiled floor. As the door slid open, he cast a lingering, eerie smile with those same dead eyes and remarked, "You sure are the prettiest thing I've ever seen." Then, he walked out into the night.

Kimberly promptly locked the door and flipped the sign to 'Closed.' She watched Zackary climb into his truck and slowly drive past the store's front windows.

Zackary's gaze remained fixed on Kimberly as he passed by. He waved, sending shivers down her spine. Nervously, she waved back before returning to her register.

Kimberly briefly considered calling her boyfriend but thought better of it; they had been in a week-long spat over his drinking, and she didn't want him to misinterpret her actions as a reconciliation attempt.

Instead, she decided to contact the sheriff's department. Picking up the phone, she hesitated and then replaced the receiver. What could she possibly report? She was scared because an unfamiliar young man had entered the store, bought some items, and left. It seemed an inadequate reason for a swift police response. Yet, the recent disappearance of a schoolteacher weighed heavily on her mind and might be enough to compel the deputies to react more urgently.

She once again lifted the receiver, dialing the sheriff's department.

"I left that store feeling on top of the world. There was a connection between that girl and me. I could tell by her tone she liked me. She even said I was sweet. I knew I would kill that pretty thing so I could be the keeper of her soul forever. I drove around to the side of the store and parked. Only one car was in the parking lot, so I figured it was hers. I decided I'd just wait until she drove home and follow her. I wasn't sure how I would get her into the truck once we got to her place, but I wanted to see where she lived before I killed her."

"I was thinking about all that stuff when headlights turned on from under a tree near the store's main entrance. And wouldn't you just know it, it was a deputy. He had been sitting there the whole time, and I didn't see him."

"The deputy pulled his patrol truck up behind me. Now I was fucked. I couldn't back out, and I couldn't drive through the store wall in front of me. If I hadn't made Jacob stay home, I was sure he would have known what to do."

"The deputy turned on his spotlight, so I couldn't see him when he got out of his car, but I heard his door shut behind him when he got out. Luckily for me, I put that knife of Daddy under the seat before I went inside the store."

"When the deputy got to my door, I looked at him and smiled like everything was fine. He started out pretty nice."

"Good evening, young man. Is there a reason you left the store, only to drive around the place and park right here?"

"No, sir.' I knew I fucked up with that stupid answer."

"You mean there is no reason you parked here?"

"Well, yes, sir, there is a reason, just not a good reason. My Momma sent me to pick up a few things for her, and I just wanted to double-check that I got everything before heading home."

"He shone his flashlight inside the truck, then looked right at me."

"Where do you live, boy?"

"I live off Highway One, at the Williams place. I'm Zackary Williams, Charlie Williams's boy."

"Is that right? Your dad doesn't come into town much, does he?"

"No, sir, he only comes around to do car work and stuff from time to time."

"I know, boy. I just haven't seen him down this way for a bit."

"I was getting nervous. I didn't know why he was asking about Daddy."

"Well, he's been busy working around the house."

"Is that right? I don't suppose you have a driver's license, do you?"

"I had a feeling this deputy would let me have it if I tried lying to him."

"No, sir, but I know how to drive. Plus, I don't go around driving anywhere but to the store, then right back home."

"He tapped his belt buckle and looked around like he was thinking about something."

"Listen, boy, I could tow this pile of shit, but I'm not going to, not tonight anyway. So what I'm going to do is have you drive straight home and not drive this thing again until you get yourself a driver's license."

"I was damn relieved. I thought he was going to send me back home on foot."

"Thank you, sir. I'll go straight home, and you won't see me ever come down this way again without my license."

"Don't thank me, son. It's just that we have other things more important going on around here. I suppose you have heard about the missing schoolteacher."

"Yes, sir, I heard a little about her."

"What did you hear, son?"

"I knew he was waiting for me to say something stupid, but I was careful."

"Well, sir, I heard she went missing. That's about it."

"That's it, you say. You heard nothing else?"

"No, sir, that's all I heard."

"So I suppose you know nothing about her missing right about where your driveway is."

"My hands started shaking a bit. It took all I had not to bust out and start running."

"No, I know nothing about that."

"No? Well, what if I told you I saw you drive right past me the other day, right near where your driveway starts? It looked like you were heading home."

"I decided I was going to run if he started in on me much more."

"Well, sir, I'm sure you saw me heading home, but that doesn't mean I know anything other than what I told you."

"Well, son, that's not the whole truth, is it? A good deputy friend of mine stopped you right as you headed up your driveway. Now, why would he tell me he talked to you and asked you if you had seen that missing teacher's car? I know he wasn't lying to me. So why would you be lying about not knowing her car was last seen right about where your driveway is?"

"I felt for the door handle. I was going to get the hell out of there, even if it meant running."

Kimberly fished her car keys out of her purse as she exited the back of the store. She double-checked the door, a responsible assistant manager's habit, and then strolled around the building to her parking spot.

To her surprise, Deputy Barnes was parked behind the boy from earlier. He had spotted her and exchanged a few words with the peculiar individual before approaching her.

Before he could speak, she preemptively inquired, "Did he do something?"

Barnes glanced back at the still-seated Zackary in the truck. "No, I just parked where I could keep an eye on your car. However, with this missing woman case, I wanted to make sure you got to your car safely."

"Thank you, Barnes. That guy was in the store just before closing. He didn't do anything strange, but he gave me the creeps. I almost called you guys twice but decided not to cry wolf."

"Listen, Kim," he said with the tone of a concerned parent. "You call us anytime you feel the need. Your father meant a lot to this town, and we owe him that much."

Barnes' words touched Kimberly deeply. Her father had been the county Sheriff for four decades, faithfully serving his community until a year ago when he died in an off-duty car accident.

"Barnes, would you mind following me home? I hate asking, but with that teacher missing, I'd feel much safer having you escort me."

Barnes offered a reassuring smile. "Of course, Kim. Let me take care of this young man, and then I'll make sure you get home safe and sound.

"I'm not sure why I didn't take off running once that deputy went over to talk to the pretty girl from the store, but looking back, I'm sure glad it didn't come to that. He would have shot me anyway."

"I watched him walk over to the girl. I don't know what they were talking about, but it looked like they knew each other. Lucky for me, when he got back to the truck, all he said was, 'You get home, son. We'll talk again soon.'"

"I didn't say it, but I was thinking, I hope we won't."

"He backed out from behind me and followed that girl out of the parking lot. They turned right, and I turned left. That was the last time I ever saw the girl. I sometimes still think about her and how I missed out on being with her when she took her last breath, but I guess that's how it goes."

"I was lucky that night. If it hadn't been for that girl showing up when she did, I'm sure I would have talked my way right into going to jail or got myself shot."

Darleen stepped back into the house, slamming the screen door behind her. Startled, Charlie looked up at her from his newspaper.

"Well, goddamn that worthless, piece-of-shit boy. I knew damn well we shouldn't let him go off at night like that. Daddy, I'm so worried I could shit myself."

Charlie walked over to Darleen and kissed her. "Now, Momma, there ain't no need to get so worked up. He ain't that late yet. Why don't we run upstairs and take care of that girl like you were talking about? You know it would make you feel better."

Although Darleen was shaking with anger, she kissed him. "All right, baby, let's do it. I've wanted to fuck that bitch up all day. She's gonna pay for what she did to me."

Charlie gently kissed her, then said, "Now you wait here, baby. I'm gonna run downstairs and get the pliers." He kissed her again and ran down into the cellar.

Darleen opened one of the kitchen drawers, sifting through her cooking utensils until she found her tongs. She put them on the table, then shuffled through her dishrags until she found a towel she didn't mind sacrificing.

Charlie ran back up the stairs, holding a pair of rusty pliers. He could hardly contain his excitement. Darleen was rarely involved with another woman. He knew he was in store for an exciting night.

"I pulled up to the house around eleven thirty. Judging by all the lights on, I knew Momma and Daddy were waiting for me. I thought about turning that truck around and leaving, but I figured I might as well just deal with what I had coming."

I heard Momma and Daddy inside laughing about something when I got to the front door. I took a deep breath, and just as I was getting ready to open the door, Jacob showed up out of nowhere. He was standing right beside me. He scared the shit out of me."

"Are you going to tell Momma and Daddy about what happened tonight?"

"I had half a mind to slap the shit out of him."

"Goddammit, Jacob, you scared me to death. What are you doing sneaking up on me like that?"

"He didn't look like he was in the mood to joke around. Instead, I could see that he was worried."

"I wasn't sneaking around, Zack. You walked right past me."

"Well, I didn't see you."

"It doesn't matter. What matters is if you plan on telling Momma and Daddy what happened tonight."

"I don't know how Jacob always knew everything I did, but he did. So I wasn't too surprised about his asking."

"I don't plan on telling them about that deputy talking to me if that's what you mean."

"That's exactly what I mean. It would be best if you didn't tell them anything about that. Just tell them you got pulled over or something and that everything turned out okay."

"I will. I'll just make up some bullshit along those lines and hope they believe it."

"Jacob still had that worried look on his face. 'Well, go on and get this over with."

"When I went in the house, Daddy was walking down the stairs ahead of Momma with a bowl in his hand. They sure seemed to be in a good mood. Well, that was until they saw me. Daddy saw me first. He stopped laughing and just stood at the bottom step. I don't know what he was thinking, but he looked like he wanted to kill me."

"Momma walked around him, taking the bowl out of his hands. She walked right up to me and said, 'See what's in this bowl? I'm going to do the same thing to you the next time you fuck up, and I'm sure that's going to be real soon."

"I looked at what she had. There were bloody teeth and a pair of pliers in the bowl. I knew where they came from."

"Daddy walked up to me, and just as he raised his hand to hit me, Momma grabbed hold of his arm. 'Not tonight, daddy. I'm in a good mood, and if I have to deal with this bullshit tonight, it's going to ruin everything."

"Daddy looked at her, surprised, but he didn't argue. Instead, he lowered his hand and walked by me toward the kitchen. That was when I saw the bloody towel hanging out of his back pocket. I knew they must have torn Miss Sarah up when I was out."

"Momma started swirling the bowl around real slow like she was thinking about what to say next. While she did that, I could hear the teeth and pliers swishing around."

"I'm sure you have a good excuse for being late, but we will not talk about that tonight. Like I told your daddy, I had a good night, and I won't have it all fucked up by you getting beat. We can deal with that in the morning."

"Then she walked right by me to the kitchen. I heard her and Daddy start laughing again, so I figured it would be best to lie on the couch and try to get some sleep."

"It wasn't long after Momma and Daddy went into their room that I heard them making that damn grunting sound. Between that and Miss Sarah moaning, I wouldn't get much sleep that night."

Killing Time

"I stayed awake on the couch until late. That night, I decided, was as good a day as any to kill Daddy and Momma. Maybe I could get Miss Sarah some help if she wasn't dead already. I also figured if I killed Momma and Daddy, I wouldn't have to deal with any more beatings. I looked down at Jacob. He was sleeping."

"Jacob, wake up, boy."

"Jacob opened his eyes and looked up at me. 'Are you ready, Zack?'"

"How did you know I was planning on doing something?"

"Jacob laughed. 'I always know what you are thinking about.'"

"You think Momma and Daddy are asleep now?"

"Jacob sat up and turned his head like he was listening hard. 'Yep, they're both asleep now."

"What about Miss Sarah? You think she's sleeping?"

"Jacob looked up at the stairs at my bedroom door. 'Yep, and if she ain't, she's keeping real quiet."

"I looked up at my door. 'Jacob, what if she hollers out when I get up there?"

"Well then, you're going to have to do like you said you would do last night. Cover her mouth up real quick. Just be really careful. Sometimes, you don't know your own strength."

"What do I do if she doesn't stop hollering?"

"Jacob kind of thought for a minute, then he said, 'Well then, you're just gonna have to run into Daddy's room and kill them."

"I don't want to get shot, Jacob."

"Then you do, like I told you last night. You kill him quickly.

"What should I use to kill them, a knife?"

"No, Daddy might get a hold of you if you don't get him in the right spot. So you need to sneak out back and grab Daddy's ax from the shed.

That way, you can hit him in the head with it. He won't have no time to do nothing then."

"All right then. Should I get the axe before I go up and talk to Miss Sarah?"

"Jacob nodded. 'That'd be the best thing. That way, if everything goes right, you won't have to go up the stairs twice. Be lucky if Daddy doesn't wake up as soon as we start up the first time."

"I glanced at the cellar, then said, 'Fine, let's go."

"I tiptoed as quietly as a mouse into the cellar and out the back door. There was no moon, so it was so damn dark out. I had to stand still for a minute to let my eyes adjust. After a minute, I sneaked on over to the shed. The door was already half open, so I just kind of turned sideways and went inside. I didn't want to mess around with that old squeaking door."

"I felt around inside a bit. After some bumping and rattling, I found the axe. It was the big one I used for chopping firewood. I took it off the wall and felt for the door. That was when Jacob said, 'Zack, stop moving. I think Daddy's awake."

"I thought I was gonna shit my pants right there. If Daddy caught me messing around outside in the middle of the night, he'd beat the living shit out of me. I listened hard, but I didn't hear Daddy. So I whispered to Jacob, 'Is he awake?"

"Jacob turned from the door and put his finger to his lips. Then he motioned for me to follow him. I hunkered down behind him, and we ran across the yard. All the while, I was looking up at Daddy's bedroom window."

"When we got into the cellar, I got close to Jacob and asked, 'Why'd you think Daddy was up?"

Jacob looked at me all wide-eyed. "I don't know. I thought I heard something; I must be a little scared, is all."

"Now, don't be saying that. I'm the one supposed to be scared. You have to be brave, or I ain't never going to do this."

"Jacob put his hand on my shoulder. 'I ain't scared, Zack. I just want this to go right, is all. Now, no more talking.'"

"We walked to the stairs, and real quiet-like, we started up. Those steps can creak loud if you don't know where to put your feet, but being as I grew up in that house, I knew exactly where to step so that they wouldn't make a sound."

"When I got to the top of the steps, I could see a dim light coming from under my bedroom door. I knew it was that damn Darth Vader light. Other than that, the only light was from the open window at the end of the hall, and that wasn't much, just a soft gray glow from a half-full moon."

"My nerves were getting the best of me. I froze up when I was about three feet away from Momma and Daddy's bedroom door."

"From behind me, Jacob whispered, 'What's the matter, Zack? You can't lose your nerve now. You're damn near past the point of no return.'"

"I glanced back at him and whispered, 'Shut your damn mouth, Jacob. You're just making things worse.'"

"That was when I heard Momma and Daddy's bed creak. I knew that sound was coming from Daddy's side of the bed. It only made that sound when Daddy got in or out of bed. Then I heard a soft bump as Daddy grabbed his gun from his nightstand. This was it. There was no turning back. I raised the axe like I was getting ready to swing a baseball bat and waited for him to come through that door."

"It's funny that I noticed every little thing around me at that moment. It was like everything was in slow motion. The doorknob twisted, then made a little pop sound. Then suddenly, Daddy came flying out of that room, swinging that gun all over the place. He didn't get far."

"He looked at the axe, then up at me. The only words he had time to say were 'What the fuck are y—'"

"Then I swung that ax with all I had. I hit him right across his stomach, damn near cutting him in half with that single blow. He fired a single round right through the floor, then fell to his knees."

"I didn't have to hit him again, but he was right there, mad as hell and gurgling something. I'm sure he was trying to call me by some bad name or something. So, anyway, I swung that ax straight down into the middle of his chest. That was when he fell onto his side, spilling guts and blood all over the place."

"I had a hell of a time pulling that ax out of his chest. It got hung up on some bone or something. I had to step on his neck and yank it out of there."

"When I turned around, Momma was standing in the doorway. She was so scared she couldn't even scream. For a second, I almost felt a little bad for her. But it was killing time, and she was next."

"She tried closing the door on me, but I was hot on her heels. She knew she had nowhere to go, so when she got to the foot of the bed, she turned to face me. I had never seen her look so scared as she did then. I think she was going to try talking her way out of it, but all she got out was 'Baby, don't kill m—'"

"Then whack. I sent the ax right across her stomach, just like I did Daddy. She fell damn near in two pieces to the floor. Then, just for good measure, I went ahead and split her chest too."

"It surprised me how easy it was to kill them. I didn't feel any regret or anything. I just stood there for a while, listening to the silence of the house. A cool draft came in through all the windows, and it was almost like the house was breathing. Looking back, maybe it was. Maybe the house was happy that I killed them."

"I stood there for a few minutes before dropping the ax beside my Momma and heading for Miss Sarah."

"There was no need for me to sneak around anymore, so I opened my bedroom door and walked in. Jacob was already there, standing beside the bed. Miss Sarah wasn't moving. Her eyes were open, and she stared straight at the ceiling."

"I asked Jacob, 'Is she dead?'"

"Jacob looked at me. I could tell it shook him up a bit."

"No, she isn't dead, but they tore her up. Look at what they did to her mouth."

"I walked over beside Jacob to have a better look. He was right. They did a job on her. Her mouth was partially open, so I could see there wasn't a tooth left. They pulled out every one of them."

"Her legs weren't in much better shape. They were red and swollen up like hot dogs. I may not be the smartest person in the world, but I knew a nasty infection when I saw it. And in that case, I could see it and smell it. Poor Miss. Sarah was rotting away in my bed."

"I untied her as carefully as I could, then picked her up. She never said a word or put up any kind of fight. She just lay limp in my arms like she was dead. I looked back at Jacob when I got to the door."

"Are you coming with me or what?"

"Are we going to the hospital?"

"Hell yes, we are, and we better get going quick before she dies."

"Jacob put his hands in his pocket and then looked out the window. 'Well, don't be surprised if we never come back here, Zack."

"What's that supposed to mean? You said all we had to do was tell everyone the truth, and we wouldn't have to go to jail."

"I know what I said. I just hope I was right."

"Well, come on, Jacob, let's go. She's in bad shape."

"Jacob followed me down the stairs. We stopped in the living room to have one last look around in case we didn't get to come back home for a while."

"That was when we saw flashing red-and-blue lights through the trees, and by the look of it, there were a lot of them coming. For a second, I thought about laying Miss Sarah down on the porch and running for it. But when that police helicopter roared over the treetops, it lit the whole place like daylight."

"I guess this is it, Jacob."

"I guess it is."

Zackary glanced at Dr. Creed, uneasy anticipation hovering in the air. "And here we are."

Allen noted the time on his watch before jotting it down in his notebook. "Yes, Zackary, indeed, we're here. I believe, for now, we'll call it a day. I have some things I need to review before scheduling our next appointment."

An edge crept into Zackary's voice as he probed further. "What things, Doctor? I've laid it all out, haven't I?"

Allen, maintaining his professional demeanor, reassured him, "I just need a little time to go over what we've discussed today so I can work on developing a treatment plan."

Zackary felt an unsettling vibe about that "treatment plan." He inquired with skepticism, "Treatment plan? What the fuck does that supposed to mean? Are you talkin' about some hypnotic shit? Or are you planning to medicate me into a zombie?"

Zackary's abrupt change in tone momentarily took aback Allen. "Zackary, I apologize if I've given you the wrong impression. I have no intention of sedating you; you haven't given me any reason to consider that necessary."

Jacob tugged at Zackary's pants leg, breaking the tension. "What the hell, Zack? You're coming off like you're crazy. You need to calm down before he thinks you're dangerous."

Zackary locked eyes with Dr. Creed. "I'm sorry, Doctor. I guess I'm just a bit tired. Maybe it's best if I go to my cell for some rest."

Allen tapped his pen on the notepad, feeling a lingering unease. He sensed he might have glimpsed a darker side of Zackary.

"I agree; we can all use some rest for the night. I'll schedule another session soon."

Allen discreetly pressed a button on his desk, summoning Woods immediately. "Woods, would you kindly escort Zackary back to his room? Our session is concluded for today."

Once Woods had left with Zackary, Allen let out a sigh of relief as the door closed. He was no fan of role-playing, and today's act had pushed his limits. Regarding sedating Zackary, he decided to postpone such measures and revisit the outburst he had witnessed.

In the meantime, he planned to schedule another session in a fortnight, providing Zackary ample time for reflection. If Zackary returned in two weeks, appearing as the pleasant young man he had been, Allen would attribute the episode to cumulative stress and prescribe mild sedatives alongside low-dose antipsychotic medication.

However, if Zackary reappeared in the next session as a madman, Allen was ready to reassess his entire treatment strategy, bringing in the heavy artillery – the zombie treatment, as it were.

Nightmares

Later that evening, Allen helped Abbey with the dishes, his thoughts consumed by fragments of Zackary's harrowing story. It wasn't until she spoke that his mental gears came to a halt.

"Allen, I think you need to go to your office. You have a lot on your mind, so go work on it."

Aware of his preoccupation and guilt for neglecting Abbey, Allen admitted, "Abbey, I'm sorry about tonight. I haven't said more than two words to you since I got home."

Abbey responded with understanding, offering a reassuring smile. "No need to apologize, Allen. I know you've got a lot on your plate."

"You're right, Abbey. My thoughts are all over the place. I think I need to work things out before bedtime." Allen quickly kissed Abbey before slipping into his office and shutting the door behind him.

Later that night, Abbey listened to Allen's muffled voice as he reviewed the recorded interview. She anticipated he would be up late, so instead of waiting up for him, she left her book on the nightstand and turned off the light.

Several hours later, Allen joined Abbey in bed, and he had made no significant progress in understanding Zackary's complex case.

In his dreams, Allen found himself standing in the illuminated living room of the Williams' house. The lights flickered ominously, casting dancing shadows on the walls, while the fire in the fireplace seemed to burn with an unnatural intensity. Country music played from an old, crackling radio upstairs; its melody twisted into a haunting tune that sent shivers down Allen's spine.

"All right, you're inside the Williams house; it's lit up, a fire is burning, and there's music. So, there's a sense of loss or helplessness, perhaps," he thought, his mind racing even in slumber. "But it's more than that; something's going to reveal itself."

As if in response to his thoughts, the music abruptly ceased, plunging the room into an eerie silence. From the darkness of the cellar below, a voice called out, low and menacing, "Dr. Creed, come down. I want to show you something."

Allen's heart quickened with dread as he approached the head of the stairs, the oppressive darkness below seeming to swallow any semblance of courage he possessed. The voice whispered again, more insistent, "Come down here, Dr. Creed."

Unease coiled in Allen's gut as he strained to see through the thick blackness, his senses alert to every creak and groan of the old house. "I can't see you. Reveal yourself," he demanded, his voice betraying his fear.

Sinister laughter echoed from the depths, chilling him to the bone. "Come down here, Dr. Creed. I won't hurt you."

A cold sweat broke out across Allen's brow as something unseen and malevolent scraped the floor behind him. He whirled around to confront the unseen menace, but a powerful force yanked his legs out from under him before he could react. With a sharp cry, he was dragged into the forbidding cellar, the darkness enveloping him like a suffocating shroud.

With a start, Allen awoke, his heart pounding in his chest, the echoes of chilling laughter still ringing in his ears. Beside him, Abbey stirred, roused by his distress. "Allen, what's wrong?" she asked, her voice filled with concern.

Though shaken to his core, Allen tried to dismiss the nightmare, his voice trembling as he replied, "It's nothing, Abbey, just a bad dream." But deep down, he knew that whatever lurked in the shadows of his subconscious was far more sinister than mere imagination.

Abbey sensed there was more to it, understanding that perhaps the stress of his career and the passage of time were taking a toll on Allen. She resolved to discuss his retirement soon.

As Abbey watched Allen drive away the following morning, she couldn't help but hope that these mornings alone were numbered. She was eager to share more of their lives together, and every day he spent at work felt like a missed opportunity.

With her second cup of coffee in hand, Abbey turned her attention to the day's chores. But a soft knock at the front door interrupted her thoughts, even though it was earlier than usual for a visitor.

As Abbey cautiously opened the door, she was taken aback by the sight of a young boy, around ten or eleven years old, sporting a John Deere baseball cap, standing on her porch.

"Well, hello there, young man. Why are you out so early?" Abbey asked, her curiosity piqued.

The boy explained his situation, "I was walking my dog this morning, and he got loose from me. I was just wondering if maybe you had seen him. His name is Sparky."

Abbey glanced up and down the street, somewhat uncertain about the circumstances. "I've never seen you before. What's your name?"

With an ear-to-ear grin, the boy replied, "My name is Jacob, ma'am, and I'm visiting my grandma. She lives about a block up the road."

Abbey nodded, "Well, Jacob, it's pretty early for a boy your age to be walking around outside."

A sinister grin crept across Jacob's lips. "For most kids, maybe, but not me. I can take care of myself, and you'll be seeing more of me around here."

Abbey felt a chill race down her spine at his words. "So, have you seen my dog or not?"

"No, Jacob, I haven't seen your dog. But give me a minute. I'll run into the kitchen and grab a pen. That way, I can jot down your number and call you if I see your dog," Abbey replied, trying to mask her unease.

Jacob winked, sending shivers down Abbey's spine. "You do that, Abbey."

As Abbey turned to head inside, she felt a sense of unease settling in the pit of her stomach. "Jacob, how did you know my name? I never told you."

Jacob's grin widened as he replied, "Yes, you did. You asked me my name, and I told you it's Jacob. Then you said your name was Abbey."

Although Abbey knew she hadn't revealed her name, she decided not to push the issue. She quickly retrieved a pen from the kitchen and returned to the porch, only to find it empty. Jacob had vanished without a trace.

Bewildered and uneasy, Abbey scanned the street, but there was no sign of the boy. Suddenly, the phone rang, startling her. She answered, and to her astonishment, Jacob's voice echoed on the other end, claiming he'd found his dog.

Abbey's heart raced as she asked Jacob how he had obtained her number, but all she received in response was a disturbing click, leaving her in an inexplicable state of dread.

Abbey couldn't ignore the bizarre circumstances. Jacob seemed to know things he shouldn't, disappearing in an unsettling manner, leaving her with a haunting sense that there was far more to this boy than met the eye.

Two weeks had passed since Allen's last session with Zackary, and he now sat at his desk, lost in thought, replaying Zackary's recent behavior in his mind. This session was an attempt to gauge Zackary's current mental state after the break.

Woods accompanied Zackary into Allen's office. Zackary's demeanor appeared more optimistic. He greeted Allen with a cheerful tone. "Good morning, Dr. Creed. How are you this morning?"

Allen responded with a chuckle, noting Zackary's improved demeanor. "I'm doing well, Zackary. You do seem to be in a better mood today."

"Why wouldn't I be, Doctor?" Zackary replied with a casual shrug. "I'm just happy to be out of my cell for a while."

"Well, I can understand that, Zackary. How have you been passing the time?" Allen inquired, luring Zackary into conversation.

Zackary sensed that Allen's question was calculated. He considered his response carefully. "I just think about how someday I'll be free again. That keeps me going."

Allen cleared his throat, broaching the sensitive topic. "Well, Zackary, that day may be quite some time away. You confessed to murdering your parents."

Zackary's voice remained measured, trying not to raise it. "So what the hell does that mean? Are you saying I may never be free? I already know what I did. I haven't tried to hide that from you."

"Now, Zackary, I didn't say you would never be free," Allen explained, treading carefully. "I said it may be quite some time before that happens. We have a lot of therapy to complete before I would even consider presenting a case for your freedom, and again, that will be quite some time away."

"Well, as long as it's not too far away, I have things I still need to do," Zackary responded with guarded optimism.

"What things, Zackary?" Allen asked, curious about his patient's aspirations.

"Nothing bad, if that's what you're thinking," Zackary replied. "I just mean, like living a normal life, starting with going back home. Who knows, Doctor, I may even start a new life and get married. You never know."

Allen found himself challenged with telling Zackary the bleak truth, the grim reality of his situation. However, he decided to let Zackary cling to a glimmer of hope. "Well, Zackary, that sounds nice. But for now, we need to focus on getting you well."

"I figured you would say something like that," Zackary responded. "If that's the case, then let's get started."

"Okay, Zackary," Allen began to discuss the topic of medication. "I think it would be best to try a different medication. I've reviewed the medication you've been prescribed, and I believe I have something that will be more effective in helping you."

Zackary stared at Allen. "Like what, some kind of shit that makes me sleep all the time because if that's the case, I won't take it, period."

"Oh, you'll take it whether or not you like it," thought Allen.

"No, nothing like that, just some better medication, that's all," Allen assured Zackary.

Zackary didn't appreciate the conversation's direction but decided arguing wouldn't serve his cause.

"Okay, Doctor, I trust you. I just don't want to sleep all the time. When I was arrested, they gave me all kinds of meds. It took all I had to stay awake. It was terrible."

"Well, enough of that for now, Zackary," Allen pivoted. "Let's discuss your feelings about what you did to your parents."

"What more do you need to know? I killed them, and I don't feel bad about it. I would do it all over again. They abused me for my entire life. Worse, Daddy killed my real Momma and Daddy."

"I understand, Zackary, but do you think you could have handled the situation differently?" Allen probed, pushing for some self-reflection.

Zackary thought for a moment, realizing he needed to backtrack a bit. "You know, Doctor, I guess I could have handled it differently. I could have run away."

"Well, there you go, Zackary. That's what I mean. There were other options. Unfortunately, you chose the wrong option, one that cost not only your parents' lives but also your freedom."

"I understand that, Doctor," Zackary replied, giving a half-hearted shrug. "I made a terrible decision."

"Yes, you did," Allen acknowledged. "But, Zackary, we all make mistakes. Unfortunately, in your case, there is no 'I'm sorry' or taking it back."

"I know that now, Doctor," Zackary replied, feigning compliance.

Allen recognized that Zackary was not sharing his true feelings or intentions during the session. An hour passed, with Zackary continuing to withhold his honest thoughts and intentions. Allen concluded the session, realizing it was unproductive. Perhaps Zackary needed more time for introspection.

As Woods wheeled Zackary out of his office, Allen overheard Zackary's conversation with Woods. "What a fucking waste of time."

Once Zackary returned to his cell and the metal door shut behind him, Jacob was waiting on his bed.

"Well, look at you, Jacob, carefree as a bird," Zackary remarked.

Jacob rolled onto his side to face Zackary. "Why would I have a care in the world? I'm not the one who thinks they're stuck here. I can leave this place and be back home in no time."

"It must be nice, Jacob, but unlike you, I can't go anywhere. I should have never listened to you. I shouldn't have killed Momma and Daddy. I told you this was going to happen."

Jacob rolled his eyes in response. "Zack, I've told you a million times you can get out of here anytime you want. You just have to concentrate on it and make it happen."

Zackary sat on the bed. "Scoot over. You're hogging the whole damn bed." Zackary looked around his tiny cell. "I know what you told me, and I can't seem to find a way out of here."

"You will, Zack, and you'll feel much better when you get out."

Zackary sighed before lying down. "I guess. Are you staying the night?"

"No, not tonight, Zackary. I have some things to get done before I go home."

"What things?"

"Just things, Zack. If you would concentrate like I've been telling you, then you could come along sometime." Zack had heard enough of Jacob's unrealistic expectations.

"Well, for now, I'm stuck here all thanks to you."

Jacob climbed over Zack. "Well, either way, I'm going to get going. I'll try seeing you tomorrow."

Zackary didn't try talking him into staying any longer. He was beginning to dislike Jacob.

Jacob walked toward the door before glancing over his shoulder. "Aren't you going to say goodbye?"

Without taking his eyes off the ceiling, Zack replied, "Bye."

That evening, Allen arrived home to find Abbey waiting on the front porch; she looked troubled.

"Abbey, what are you doing out here?"

Abbey opened the front door ahead of Allen. "Right after you left, I had the strangest visitor."

"A visitor?"

"A little boy I've never seen before came to the door asking if I had seen his dog."

"Now that is a strange visitor. How old was he?"

"I didn't ask, but he couldn't have been more than eleven. He said his name was Jacob, and he was staying at his grandmother's house. Allen, he knew my name. He called me Abbey. I never told him my name."

Allen set his briefcase on the kitchen table. "Jacob? 'This has got to be a complete coincidence," he thought.

"It gets even odder. I went to the kitchen to get a pen, and when I returned, he was gone. A few minutes later, he called here, telling me he found his dog. Allen, I never gave him our number, and he could not walk a block to his grandma's house that quickly."

Allen felt a chill run down his spine. "What was the little boy wearing?"

"Blue jeans and a white T-shirt, why?"

"Was he wearing a baseball cap?"

"Yes," Abbey responded suspiciously. "Allen, do you know who the boy is?"

"Abbey, as you know, Zackary Williams is a patient of mine. Without going into specific detail, he has an imaginary friend named Jacob. And according to Zackary, his friend always wears a John Deere baseball cap."

Abbey sat beside Allen. "You said 'imaginary friend.'"

"Yes, there has to be an explanation. I'm sure it's just a strange coincidence. There is no other way of explaining it," said Allen.

Abbey took hold of Allen's hand. "Do you think we should call the police?"

Allen thought for a moment. "No, there's nothing to tell them. Once you explain what happened this morning, all they'll do is take some notes and leave."

"I suppose you're right; they would think I had lost my mind."

"I know you have. I knew it when you accepted my marriage proposal," Allen laughed. "No calling the police yet."

That night, Abbey's heart raced as she struggled to catch her breath in the suffocating darkness of their bedroom. The bedroom door was open, an unsettling departure from her nightly routine of securely sealed solitude. She shivered, her fingers trembling as she reached out for Allen.

Just as her fingertips brushed his chest, a figure emerged from the shadowy depths of their closet. It was Jacob; gone was the facade of childish innocence that had initially masked Jacob's sinister presence. He leered at Abbey, his eyes gleaming with malice. A spine-chilling shiver coursed down Abbey's spine as his malevolent gaze bore into her soul. Jacob bolted from the room with a final, menacing glare, his laughter echoing in the darkness.

Allen jolted awake, his voice heavy with confusion and concern, "What's going on, Abbey?" he asked, sitting up beside her.

Tears welled up in Abbey's eyes as she stammered, "Allen, get up. Jacob was in our room. He ran out when he knew I saw him."

Allen quickly pulled the blankets back, picking up his baseball bat before searching the house.

The house was enveloped in eerie silence; only one room remained unchecked—Allen's dimly lit office. With trembling hands, he cautiously pushed open the door, his heart pounding in his chest. His breath caught as he was confronted with a surreal sight: a little boy, no older than eleven, sat perched on the edge of his cluttered desk. The boy wore a sinister grin that contrasted with his cherubic features.

"Hello, Dr. Creed," the boy chirped, his voice dripping with innocence yet tainted by an unmistakable malevolence.

Allen's eyes darted around the room, scanning for an escape route. His voice quivered as he demanded answers, "Who are you? How did you get into my house?"

The boy's grin remained unshaken. "Dr. Creed, come in and close the door. I have something to tell you."

Reluctantly, Allen complied, shutting the door behind him. "Listen, I am calling the police. So whatever you have to say, do it quickly."

"The police?" Jacob chuckled, his laughter sending chills down Allen's spine. "Dr. Creed, I won't be here when they show up."

"Yes, you will. I won't let you out," Allen declared, mustering the last remnants of his dwindling courage.

Jacob rolled his eyes, "Anyway, I thought you should know that Abbey has been talking to her friends. She says you are a confused old man, and she intends to divorce you and take everything you have."

Allen's laughter resonated with disbelief. "Oh, is that right? So tell me, Jacob, do you have anything else to say before I call the police?"

Jacob responded with an air of calm, "Yup, I sure do, Dr. Creed. Why don't you ask Abbey whom she spends her time with when you're at work?"

Intrigued and unnerved, Allen cautiously stepped toward the evil child. "What are you talking about?"

Jacob grinned, "You know what I'm talking about."

Confused, Allen smirked, "I've heard enough of this. I'm calling the police!" Allen reached for his phone.

"Go ahead, call them," Jacob taunted. "What will you tell them when they get here? A little boy was in your house and then vanished?"

"Look behind you, Dr. Creed."

Allen glanced over his shoulder, his heart racing, but nothing was there. He turned back to where Jacob had been seated, only to find the desk empty. Panic welled up inside him. Allen desperately searched his office, then scoured his entire home. Jacob had vanished without a trace.

Defeated, Allen returned to his office. Perhaps the police would deem him insane for this bizarre story. He called out, "Abbey, I need your help. I'm calling the police. You must tell them you saw Jacob as well."

Abbey sat up. "Allen, what are you talking about, and why do you have that bat?"

"Abbey, Jacob, the boy you saw, I saw him too. He was in the office. I talked to him," Allen stammered. "You woke me up telling me you had seen him in our room."

Abbey shook her head. "Allen, you must have had another nightmare. I didn't see Jacob, and I didn't wake you."

Allen sat at the foot of the bed. "Abbey, I saw him. I talked to him. He was in my office."

"Allen, that is enough. You had a bad dream. If anyone came into the house, the alarm would have been triggered. Allen, you need to go back to sleep, and you need to retire. You have been acting strange. It's time, Allen. You are not the young man you used to be. Your work is taking a serious toll on you mentally."

Allen lay down beside Abbey. "It was so real, Abbey. I don't know how it could have been a dream."

"Well, it was. Now go to sleep."

Allen lay in bed replaying the entire event. It couldn't have been a dream, and what did Abbey mean by I'm not a young man anymore, and I'm acting strange? Maybe it had been a dream, but Jacob said Abbey had told her friends I'm a confused old man. If it were a dream, there were things said that rang true in Jacob's remarks.

Allen didn't go back to sleep. Instead, his mind raced as he tried to self-analyze himself. He was unraveling.

Slipping

The next morning, Allen found himself drawn to Zackary's case file. He meticulously examined the photographs of the Williams property, each image ingraining itself in his mind like a dark siren's call. There was an inexplicable, gnawing desire to see the place for himself, to walk through the halls that had witnessed such horrors. It was an irrational itch that begged to be scratched, a morbid curiosity that refused to be silenced.

Staring out of his office window, Allen was suddenly jolted from his reverie by the realization that over two hours had slipped by unnoticed. He had mentally traversed every room of the Williams house repeatedly as if the very building was summoning him. "Get a hold of yourself, old man," he muttered, trying to shake off the strange trance. "There are other matters that demand your attention."

Exiting his office, Allen resolved to put the unsettling thoughts Jacob had planted firmly to rest. He needed to verify the truth about Abbey's activities in his absence. While he considered calling her, the desire to catch her in the act drove him to check in person.

As he arrived back in his neighborhood, he immediately noticed the absence of Abbey's car in the driveway. A sense of disquiet settled in. Nothing seemed amiss inside their home, but Allen's unease refused to wane. "This is insane, but is it?" he pondered. "Abbey always texts when she's out. Something's not right."

Without hesitation, he decided to drive through town in search of Abbey. His knowledge of her favorite spots led him to a familiar sight: Abbey, seated in the front patio area of Laura's coffee shop.

At first glance, nothing appeared unusual. But then he saw him – a well-dressed man in his mid-forties approaching her table. Abbey looked up from her laptop and smiled, hugging the man tightly. A surge of anger began to simmer within Allen.

Allen's mind was a whirlwind of disbelief and betrayal as he grappled with the knowledge of Abbey's secret rendezvous with a younger man. He had provided her with everything she might desire, yet she had been meeting someone else behind his back. A wave of anger and confusion surged through him.

But just as he was about to delve deeper into his thoughts, the impatient blare of a car horn from behind momentarily broke the chains of his introspection. He hastily refocused, realizing that the traffic light had turned green. As he sped through the intersection, he noticed Abbey in his rearview mirror. She was looking in his direction.

Cursing the impatient driver who had honked his horn needlessly, Allen reflected on how Abbey might never have known he was there if not for the interruption.

His phone chimed; it was Abbey calling. Allen hesitated before answering, torn between the truth and the desire to keep his earlier actions a secret from her. He had never lied to her before, and now he faced a moral dilemma.

"Good morning, Abbey," he greeted her cautiously.

"Good morning, Allen. Hey, quick question. I'm here at Laura's with a friend of mine. I could have sworn I just saw you."

Allen chuckled. "No, not me. I've been in the office all morning."

"Okay, well, listen, I have to get off the phone. I'm a little busy now. I'll see you tonight," Abbey replied, her voice hinting at a haste that piqued Allen's curiosity.

Before he could inquire further, Abbey had already hung up, leaving Allen with a choice. Should he admit to his earlier actions and the lie, or should he remain silent and gather more information before confronting the situation?

As Allen entered his Churchill office, the phone rang once more. He sat at his desk, answering, "Good morning, this is Dr. Creed."

"It's not a good morning, is it, Doctor?" a voice on the other end taunted.

Allen recognized the voice immediately; it was Jacob. "Who is this?" he asked, feigning ignorance.

"Come on, Doctor. Don't play games. You know who this is. I told you Abbey was spending time with someone else. He's half your age, Doctor, and to put it like Abbey, he's not old and confused."

"I'm not old and confused, Jacob. There is a reasonable explanation for all this," Allen stammered, attempting to grasp rationality. "I don't know why I'm discussing with someone who is not real. This is nothing more than a temporary mental crisis related to stress."

Jacob's sinister laughter echoed in Allen's ears, casting doubt on his conviction that none of this was real. "What are you talking about? This is not real, and you are not real."

Jacob continued to taunt him. "Oh, but I am, Doctor, and you will soon face a tough decision. Oh, by the way, ask Zack to show you where Daddy and I were buried." With those chilling words, Jacob abruptly hung up the phone.

As the call ended, Allen slowly surveyed his office. He was now entangled in a web of inexplicable events, and there was no one he could confide in. To speak of this with anyone would shatter his professional reputation. He resolved to bury these unsettling thoughts deep within the recesses of his mind and press on. Allen carefully set the phone down, his hands trembling.

Shortly after hanging up, a familiar knock at his door disrupted his uneasy thoughts. Woods announced, "Dr. Creed, I have Mr. Williams here to see you."

Zackary entered, wearing a disconcertingly friendly smile. "Hello, Doctor. I suppose it's time for another round of therapy."

Allen struggled to maintain his professional composure. He had cultivated a deep loathing for Zackary since his life had been upended after being assigned to the young man.

"Hello, Zackary," Allen replied, tapping his pen on the desk. "Listen, Zackary, this session was not scheduled, but I have a few things I would like to discuss with you."

Zackary's smile remained fixed. "Okay, like what?"

"Zackary, are you positive Jacob had your best interests in mind as you were growing up?"

Zackary gave a casual shrug. "I think he did, but there are times, especially lately, that I wonder if he had me do things I shouldn't have. I sometimes think Jacob is evil and that he only took on the form of my brother, so I would trust him."

"I was thinking something along those lines as well. Zackary, would you have killed your parents had it not been for Jacob?"

"I don't know for sure. I mean, I wanted to, but he kind of pushed the issue toward the end."

Allen contemplated whether he should disclose his own disturbing experiences with Jacob visiting him, but ethical boundaries held him back. Revealing that he was experiencing the same delusions as a psychotic patient would undoubtedly legitimize Zackary's actions, and that was a risk he couldn't take.

"Zackary, would you say most of what Jacob told you was the truth?"

Zackary nodded earnestly. "Yes, Doctor, Jacob knows things, sees things, and comes up with ways to take care of an issue before it gets out of hand," Zackary observed Allen closely. "Doctor, why all the questions about Jacob?"

Allen set his pen down, concealing his inner turmoil. "No particular reason. I simply wanted to learn more about Jacob."

Zackary's gaze bore into him, suspicion evident in his eyes. "You saw him, didn't you, Doctor?"

The question startled Allen. "What? No, Zackary, I have not seen Jacob. That would be impossible. He lives in your mind and nowhere else."

"Doctor, if you see Jacob, listen to what he tells you. Just remember his way of solving problems is permanent."

Allen forced a smile. "I'll keep that in mind. Zackary, when you say he may have taken the shape of your brother, did he stay in a child's form as you grew up? Or did he appear to age like you?"

"He aged just like me."

"So where is Jacob now?"

"Who knows? He never tells me. He's been doing that more and more lately. Sometimes I won't see him for days."

"Do you ask him where he goes?"

"Sometimes." Zackary knew this was some kind of psychiatrist mind game about to unfold.

"Does he tell you?"

"Sometimes. Why?"

Allen wanted to respond, "Because now he's messing with me," but he held his tongue. "I'm just curious, Zackary. I know how close you two are. I find it odd that Jacob is staying away for longer periods and not explaining why."

Oh, here we go again, thought Zackary. "Dr. Creed, it's not a big deal. He's got things he needs to take care of. He's not the one locked up. I am."

"I understand they locked you up, not him. I guess I'm just confused."

Zackary shrugged. "I guess so."

"Okay, Zackary, enough of this Jacob discussion."

Zackary smiled. "Doctor, is that why you brought me here today? So we could talk about Jacob?"

"Actually, that is not why I brought you here today. I brought you here because you had mentioned Jacob showed you where he and your father were buried."

"I mentioned something about that." This was leading to something Zackary would have to stay one step ahead of Dr. Creed.

"Zackary, if I showed you a map of your property, do you think you could point out where the bodies are buried?"

"Probably not, Doctor. That was a while back when Jacob showed me. So why does it matter where they're buried?"

"It matters because your father's and Jacob's remains have never been recovered. I'm sure your family would like to have them so they could give them a proper funeral."

Zackary wished Jacob would show up and help him. He didn't know if he should discuss this topic without Jacob knowing about it.

Allen watched Zackary; it was apparent the subject of the burial site was bothering him. "Zackary, how about this? How about I show you a satellite map of your property? Perhaps that will help you remember."

"Give me a minute, Doctor. I'm thinking," quipped Zackary.

"Dammit, boy, where the hell are you?" Zackary wondered.

Zackary is hiding something, Allen thought.

Zackary squirmed in his chair before resigning to the fact that Jacob was not coming to help him.

"Okay, Doctor, let me have a look at the map."

Allen opened the top drawer of his desk. He slid the map toward Zackary. "Here it is. Take your time."

"Doctor, you said the family wants the remains so they can have a proper funeral for them?"

"Yes, I did. I don't feel that is an unreasonable request, do you?"

"No, I guess not, but what about my momma's remains? Last I heard, she was at the bottom of the pond."

"Zackary, they recovered your mother's remains, but they haven't been released from the coroner's office yet."

Zackary didn't think that made much sense, but then again, he thought nothing about his situation made sense. Zackary looked closely at the map. The house, shed, and ponds were easy enough to see. However, the area where Jacob had taken him was hidden beneath a canopy of trees. But just as he was going to tell Dr. Creed that he couldn't find the spot, he noticed what appeared to be an overgrown road.

He focused intently on the faint trail leading from Highway 1 into the woods before it disappeared beneath the canopy of trees.

Allen watched Zackary intently. For several minutes, Zackary's eyes were scanning the map erratically. Finally, they stopped; he recognized something. Allen waited patiently for Zackary to confirm what he suspected.

Allen knew he had found the road. He glanced at Dr. Creed; he was staring at him. Zackary didn't like his expression. He resembled a dog expecting a treat. Zackary had other plans.

Zackary straightened his back as he looked away from the map. "I can't find it, Doctor." Zackary relished the look on Dr. Creed's face. Bad dog, no treat.

Allen glanced at the map before looking at Zack. He is lying. "Zackary, are you sure you can't find it?"

"No, Doctor, I would have to be there to find it."

So that was the ploy; Zackary wanted to go on a field trip. Allen was reasonably certain he could pull some strings and make it happen. Investigators would turn down the opportunity to close two more missing person reports.

"Zackary, let's pretend for a moment that I could arrange to take you to the property. You understand it would be under heavy police supervision. It would not be just you and me out there."

"I know, Dr. Creed, but as I said, I can't find the spot without being there."

That was not the response Allen had hoped for. Instead, he thought Zackary might change his mind once he knew there would be a heavy police presence.

"Okay, Zackary, as I said earlier, this was not a scheduled session. I have to make some phone calls."

Zackary was disappointed. He was disappointed with the length of the session, and now he had to go back to his cell. Allen pressed the hidden button.

As Woods wheeled Zackary out the door, Zackary glanced over his shoulder. "Doctor, when is my next appointment?"

"It won't be long, Zackary. I will have someone bring you to me soon."

Allen neatly packed his briefcase before leaving his office for the day. As he walked toward the front doors, he glanced into the office of Theodor Fox, the human resource director of Churchill.

Allen caught fragments of the phone conversation Mr. Fox was engaged in. "I know, but that is age discrimination. At least he still shows up. I can't say the old guy isn't trying."

Allen had a sinking feeling the discussion was regarding him. They were planning some sort of strategic way of getting rid of him. "I'll show them I'm still useful. Zackary will show us where Jacob and his father were buried. They will hail me as a hero for solving that part of the puzzle. Then I'll retire on my terms, not theirs."

Allen pulled into his driveway. He glanced at the living room window. Abbey wasn't there. She always greeted him when he came home. As Allen entered the front door, he heard Abbey talking on the phone; she was in their bedroom. He placed his briefcase on the couch before silently stepping to the half-open door.

"Roger, that sounds great. I can meet you tomorrow. No, Allen doesn't suspect a thing. As usual, he has been wrapped up with his work. However, he is in for one heck of a surprise. I can hardly wait to see his face when this happens."

When what happens? When you drop the bomb by telling me you are leaving me for another man? Allen had to outsmart her. He would not let Abbey make a fool out of him by running off with another man. "I'll kill both of them before I let that happen," Allen was shocked by what he was thinking. He loved Abbey more than he had ever loved before, and now she, like everyone else, seemed to turn on him.

Allen walked back to the front door, opening it before closing it behind him as if he had just arrived home. Allen heard Abbey in the bedroom tell Roger, "He's home, Roger. I have to go. I'll call you tomorrow."

Abbey kissed Allen as she walked past him into the kitchen. "I'm going to make dinner. How was your day, Allen?"

Allen cringed. "My day was good. How was yours?"

Abbey glanced at Allen as she poured two glasses of wine.

"Oh, it was pretty uneventful."

"Hmm, pretty uneventful. Must be nice."

"It was nice, Allen. If you would retire, we could spend some uneventful time together."

Allen struggled to control his anger. "Abbey, I am almost finished dealing with Mr. Williams. I have one more task to complete, and then it's over."

Abbey handed Allen his glass of wine. "I'm looking forward to that, Allen."

That night, Allen found himself standing outside Zackary's bedroom door in a dream. The house was eerily silent, and the shadows danced ominously, casting grotesque shapes upon the walls. In the dimness, Allen could faintly discern the bloodied corpse of Charlie lying twisted in the hallway, his lifeless eyes staring into the abyss.

With trepidation, Allen reached out for Zackary's door, his heart pounding with dread. He pushed it open gently, the hinges creaking in protest. Inside, on the bed, lay Zackary, his body mangled and drenched in blood. A gaping wound on the side of his head oozed with brain matter, staining the pillow crimson.

A sense of horror washed over Allen as he backed out of the room, his knuckles grazing painfully against the doorframe. With a jolt, he realized he clutched an ax with his right hand, its metal glinting wickedly in the dim light. With a gasp of terror, Allen dropped the weapon and fled down the stairs.

But as he passed the cellar, a chilling sound echoed from below—a man's laughter, cold and mocking. The voice hissed his name, sending shivers down Allen's spine. "Dr. Creed, what have you done?"

The laughter pursued him as he burst out of the front door, his breath ragged and labored. His eyes widened in terror as he looked up, only to find a woman clinging upside down to the porch's roof, her dark hair cascading like tendrils of shadow. She moved towards him with unnatural agility, crawling on all fours like a demonic creature.

With a primal scream, Allen fled into the darkness, his mind reeling with terror and confusion. The laughter followed him, echoing in his ears as he disappeared into the night, consumed by fear and madness.

Abbey woke, startled by the commotion. Beside her, Allen was yelling something in his sleep. She shook him, trying to pull him from the grip of his nightmare. "Allen, wake up." He stirred but didn't wake. "Allen, wake up!" she yelled, urgently shaking him.

Allen's eyes fluttered open, but he was still trapped in the horrors of his dream. He stared at Abbey with wide, frightened eyes before screaming in terror. Panicked, he flailed wildly at Abbey, his fists connecting with her shoulder, and then he fell off the bed. Abbey was terrified, her shoulder throbbing with pain. She pulled the blankets back and ran for the bedroom door. Behind her, she heard Allen.

"Abbey, what happened?"

Abbey returned to the bedroom, holding her shoulder. She grabbed her pillow, ready to defend herself. "What happened? How about you tell me?"

Allen stood from the floor, rubbing the side of his head. He was disoriented. "I had a bad dream, that's all."

"No, Allen, that's not all. You were swinging at me before you threw yourself out of bed."

"I did what?" Allen was bewildered. He had never reacted like this before.

"You swung at me, Allen. I don't know what you have going on at work, but it's screwing with your mind. I won't put up with this," Abbey shouted.

Allen knew he had reached a breaking point. "I have a few things to finish up at work, and then I will submit my retirement paperwork."

"Well, I'll sleep in the guest room while you're finishing up," Abbey said firmly, her voice filled with disappointment and concern. She left the room, slamming the door behind her.

Allen lay in the dark for several hours, wrestling with his thoughts and the torment of his nightmares. The guilt of failing to protect his marriage haunted him.

As he locked the front door of the house and walked to his car, Jacob sat up in the back seat, a sinister smile on his face. Allen's heart raced, and he stomped on the brake pedal, causing the tires to chirp loudly.

"What the hell are you doing in my car?" Allen demanded, his voice trembling with fear.

Jacob continued to smile. "Doctor, keep driving before the neighbors see you talking to yourself. They already think you're insane. No need to add fuel to the fire."

Allen sighed, both relieved and distressed, as he slowly drove on. "Jacob, I don't believe my neighbors think I'm insane."

"Oh, but they do. So do your coworkers, Abbey, and her little friend, Roger."

Allen glanced in his rear-view mirror, his nerves on edge. Jacob was smirking.

"I don't care what Roger thinks of me."

"You should. That was his angle to get to Abbey. He convinced her you are too old and senile for a beautiful woman like her, and unfortunately for you, she believes him."

"Well, Jacob, I'm going to devise a plan to get rid of Roger."

"I already have a plan, Doctor."

"Oh, and what is that, Jacob?"

"Kill him."

"That seems to be your way of solving things, but it's not mine. I have no intentions of killing anyone."

"So instead, you're going to allow that man to sleep with your wife in your house?" Jacob laughed, his words dripping with malice.

As Allen parked his car in his designated spot at Churchill, he continued his unsettling conversation with Jacob. The office building loomed around him, its sterile and mundane exterior contrasting with the darkness of his thoughts.

"Don't think for a minute the two of them aren't having a great time making plans to rid you of their lives. Shit, they have already put their plan in motion. Abbey has convinced her friends and family that you are losing it. I wouldn't be surprised if she also reached out to your coworkers. So far, they are way ahead of you," Jacob taunted.

Allen took a deep breath, trying to regain his composure. "Jacob, I know you have extrasensory perception, and to a certain degree, I appreciate what you are telling me, but killing someone would lead to incarceration for the rest of my life."

"So you aren't so concerned with killing Roger as you are with spending the rest of your life in prison."

Allen thought momentarily, his hands trembling slightly on the steering wheel. "I suppose that's it. But unfortunately, the personal consequences of such drastic measures far outweigh the benefits."

"Doctor, when you are ready to kill Roger, do it in front of Abbey. Let her watch as her lover bleeds out before her while you stand the victor."

"You make it sound so easy. You tempt me. You do," chuckled Allen, a twisted edge to his laughter. "I'll have to do some serious thinking on that one."

"Then do some serious thinking."

Allen glanced over his shoulder, but Jacob had vanished, leaving him alone with his dark thoughts in the parking lot.

Zackary, confined in his cell, stared at the steel door that separated him from the outside world. The dim orange glow from a scratched plexiglass window above his bed barely illuminated his surroundings. His mind was a turbulent sea of conflicting emotions.

"Well, this is fucking great. If I wasn't insane before they put me here, I will be soon enough," he muttered to himself.

As he lay on the narrow, uncomfortable bed, Zackary let his mind drift, counting the numerous paint chips clinging to the ceiling. He thought about his life before that fateful night when he killed his parents.

I shouldn't have killed Momma and Daddy. I should have just taken the beatings when they came and let them do whatever the hell they wanted with Miss Sarah. Now look at the shit I'm in. This is the end of the road. I'll never set foot outside these walls, a free man again.

A wave of overwhelming anger welled within Zackary, like a monstrous force awakening from the depths of his psyche. It threatened to consume him.

A sudden pounding on the cell door jolted him from his dark reverie.

"Mr. Williams, Dr. Creed wants to see you. Are you good with that?" The voice belonged to Officer Woods.

Hell, yes, Zackary was good with that. He would have welcomed any opportunity to escape the confines of his cell, even if just for a few minutes. "Yes, Officer Woods, I'm good with that."

The tension in the room was palpable as Zackary was wheeled into Allen's office by Officer Woods. Allen acknowledged Zackary's presence but was visibly preoccupied with his thoughts.

"Hi, Dr. Creed," Zackary greeted Allen, hoping for answers or at least some relief from his current confinement.

Woods, the ever-watchful officer, briefly shifted his attention from Zackary to Dr. Creed. It was a routine procedure, the kind they had performed many times. "Anyway, Officer Woods, like I said, if they ever let me out of here, I'll show you my house," Zackary continued.

Woods remained professional but cordial. "That sounds nice, Mr. Williams."

Zackary smiled, "You can call me Zack or Zackary, whichever name suits you."

"Okay, Zack," Officer Woods replied, friendly and polite.

Then, following standard protocol, Woods turned to Allen. "Dr. Creed, do you want me to stand by?"

Allen, preoccupied with his thoughts, replied with a sigh. "No, Woods, make yourself comfortable in the hall."

"I'll talk to you later, Woods," Zackary said, acknowledging the officer as he left the room.

Alone with Zackary, Allen leaned forward and attempted to address the matter at hand. "Well, Zackary, by the looks of things, you are making friends."

"Yes, I have, Dr. Creed, and honestly, I feel much better."

"Well, that's good to hear, Zackary," Allen responded with a forced smile. There was something more significant he needed to discuss.

Allen gazed at Zackary, unsure how to proceed, "Zackary, I have something to tell you. I wasn't going to, but I don't think there is any reason to hide it from you. Jacob, he talked to me."

Allen's revelation took Zackary by surprise. He had never expected to hear of someone else encountering Jacob, let alone talking to him. "What did he talk to you about?" Zackary inquired, keen to know more about this extraordinary occurrence.

"He never lets people see him, let alone talk to him. He only talks to me," Zackary clarified.

"I started seeing him a while ago. We have discussed little, but he has advised me on a few topics," Allen admitted hesitantly.

Zackary's words were filled with a touch of caution and concern. "Remember what I said, Doctor. Jacob knows things, but his solution to some problems is final."

"I am aware of that. Case in point, you killed your parents," Allen acknowledged.

"Yes, like that," Zackary agreed, almost as if he were proud of Jacob's involvement.

"I intend to continue making my own decisions. I did not ask for, nor do I require, advice from Jacob. I will resolve my issues as I always have," Allen stated confidently, his tone reflecting his determination.

Zackary smiled, knowing Allen would soon understand the relentless nature of Jacob's involvement. "It may not be that easy. Jacob doesn't care whether you ask for his advice. Once he decides he is going to help you, he will not give up."

"That's fine. All the same, I can deal with my issues," Allen insisted. He did not want to concede any further ground in this strange conversation with Zackary.

Zackary was intrigued by the prospect of their next subject.

"Anyway, I brought you in for this brief session to inform you where we are regarding taking you to your property. I made a phone call to lead homicide detective Dearborn. Now the ball is in his court. I'm confident we should hear from him any day now."

Zackary was filled with excitement at the prospect of revisiting his property. "You mean we might go to my house?"

"Now, Zackary, I doubt you will be allowed inside your house. I'm sure you will be limited to escorting a team of detectives to the burial site and then returning here," Allen clarified, tempering Zackary's expectations.

Zackary's enthusiasm was somewhat deflated, but he still held onto hope. "Well, Doctor, maybe they will let me go inside quickly just to look around."

Allen, choosing not to shatter Zackary's hopes, decided to entertain the possibility. "Well, I guess we shall see. Perhaps they will let you quickly look around before we leave."

"Oh, that would be great. Let me know as soon as they call you. I can't wait to see my house again," Zackary eagerly implored.

"You have my word, Zackary. I will notify you as soon as I hear anything. But for now, I have another patient to see. We will be in touch. I promise you that much," Allen reassured him.

As Officer Woods began to wheel Zackary out of the room, Zackary couldn't help but remind him, "Doctor, don't forget to let me know as soon as you hear anything."

"It won't be long, Zackary. I will have someone bring you to me soon," Allen assured him, aware of the importance of keeping Zackary informed and managing his expectations.

In the dimly lit room, Zackary nervously looked at Jacob, whose presence was both comforting and unsettling.

"Zack, I've got something to tell you," Jacob began in a grave tone.

Zackary, intrigued and somewhat apprehensive, leaned in to listen.

"Zack, it doesn't matter whether you think you're alive or dead," Jacob continued. "There's a way for you to leave and go back home."

Zackary was skeptical and confused. "Jacob, I don't understand. This does not make any sense. I can't just leave and go back home."

Jacob sighed and explained, "Yes, you can, Zack; you can walk right through these walls if you accept that you have changed."

Zackary was reluctant to accept what he was hearing. "So, you're saying I have to give up on being alive and accept that I'm...what, dead? A ghost?"

Jacob nodded, his expression intense. "In a sense, yes. You have to let go of your attachment to the world you once belonged to. Embrace the fact that you're not what you used to be."

Zackary's mind was racing, "How can I do that?"

Jacob's voice softened. "I know it's not easy, Zack. It's a difficult choice to make. But if you stay here, you'll lose everything, including your connection to your old life. You'll become one of those who are stuck. I've seen it happen too many times. You need to decide what you want to do."

Zackary sat in contemplative silence. The weight of Jacob's words hung heavy in the air. The decision ahead was not just about life and death and embracing a new reality, even if it meant letting go of the past.

Endgame

A week had passed since Allen made the call to lead homicide detective Jack Dearborn. He understood the complexities of taking a convicted murderer to a crime scene, but he had anticipated some form of communication or an update. Frustration led him to pick up his phone and make another call.

"Homicide, this is Detective Dearborn," came the voice on the other end.

"Good morning, Dearborn; this is Dr. Allen Creed," Allen began.

"Oh yes, Dr. Creed, it's been a while. How have you been?"

Allen responded, "I'm calling regarding my patient Zackary Williams. I was wondering if there are any updates regarding bringing him to the property."

Dearborn was silent for a moment, "I'm not sure what you are referring to."

"I'm sorry, Dearborn, I thought we discussed this last week," Allen stated.

"Uh, no, we didn't," replied Dearborn.

Allen began to feel a sinking sensation. He needed to rectify the situation before Dearborn assumed he was losing his sanity. "Sure we did. I told you that Zackary will take us to where his father and brother were buried."

"Dr. Creed, we never discussed Zackary Williams or buried bodies,"

With a sense of alarm, Allen tried to regain his composure. "I apologize, Dearborn. It seems with my current workload, I've been swamped. I intended to call you, but it must have slipped my mind."

"It slipped your mind?" Dearborn's doubt was evident.

Pretending not to hear the question, Allen pressed on. "I met with Zackary last week. He told me he would take us to where the bodies were buried. I tried having him point to the location on a map, but he said he—"

Dearborn interrupted, setting Allen's panic into motion. "You met with Mr. Williams? Dr. Creed, the bodies of Williams's brother and father have already been recovered."

The realization that he had been speaking in a delusional state gripped Allen, rendering him momentarily speechless. He stammered,

"That's right. I recall seeing something about that in Zackary's case file. Your team discovered the bodies during your initial investigation."

Dearborn's voice held a patient tone as he asked, "No, Doctor, we discovered them after Mr. Williams told us where to find them. Our canine handlers worked a cadaver dog at the location and confirmed Mr. Williams's story."

Allen fell into silence, struggling to find the right words.

"Hello? Hello, Dr. Creed, are you still there?" Dearborn inquired.

Clearing his throat, Allen composed himself and replied, "Oh yes, I apologize, Dearborn. I remember reading that now."

"Okay, Doctor, is there anything else I can do for you?" Dearborn inquired, his concern evident.

"No, I appreciate you clearing that up for me. I've been busy working on a few cases. I suppose I got a few things mixed up. You have a great day, Dearborn."

"You do the same, Dr. Creed." Dearborn hung up the phone. Allen looked around his office. It was time to retire. How could he have conjured up a story regarding his first call to Dearborn? He was losing it. He had one more call to make.

As usual, Abe picked up on the second ring.

"Hello, this is Abraham Goldberg. How may I be of help?"

Allen tried to act as if nothing was wrong. "Hello there, old friend. It's Allen."

"Well, it's been a long time since I last heard from you. How have you been?"

"I've been better. I think it's time to hang up and retire. You know, pass the ole hat to my predecessor."

"Good for you, Allen. It's time to live."

"Agreed, but that is not why I called."

"Oh, well, what is it? Is everything all right? You sound a little off."

Allen thought he was doing a decent job hiding his emotions.

"Yes, everything is great. I just wanted to discuss a few things regarding my patient Zackary."

"You meant to say your almost patient."

Allen felt nauseous. "Yes, my almost patient."

"I apologize, Allen. I should have explained the mix-up to you a few months ago."

"Mix-up?"

"Yes, the mix-up. He was never supposed to be housed at Churchill. But unfortunately, the officials at Patton State Hospital called just before we prepared to send him to you."

"Oh, that's why he never showed up." Allen's head was swimming.

"Allen, I called your facility. Admissions told me they would pass a message on to you."

"Oh, it was. It just slipped my mind. You know, I think retirement is sounding better by the moment."

"I agree, Allen. It's not like you to have anything slip your mind. But what happened to Zackary is a shame. The kid may have been a train wreck, but I could have been wrong."

Allen didn't know what Abe was talking about. "Abe, I didn't bother following up on the Williams case. I had my plate full."

"He's dead, Allen. He hung himself two weeks after he arrived at Patton."

Allen couldn't speak; he had met with Zackary in this very office. He had audio and video recordings to prove it. *That's it. I'll play the video.*

"Listen, Abe; I have to get off the phone. I have another patient waiting at the door."

"Oh, okay, Allen. Well, call me. I'm a little worried about you."

"I will, Abe. I'll talk to you later."

Allen scrambled; he opened his laptop, searching for the video recording of his interview with Zackary. He scanned through the files. *Ah, there you are.* Allen opened the file (Zackary Williams).

Allen watched himself walk from behind his desk to the door. He opened it, talking to someone who was not there. In horror, he watched and listened to himself ask Woods to wait outside. He watched as he introduced himself to Zackary, only to find there was no Zackary or Woods, just an empty room. He was talking to no one. He fast-forwarded the video. Zackary was never there.

Allen closed the video, frantically searching for another. Finally, he found it (Zackary's map). He played the video. Again, there was no Zackary, just him talking to no one.

Allen logged into the facility census report. He scanned through it twice. There was no Zackary Williams. *Shit, I've lost my mind. One last try. I'll look up the employee census. If I find Woods, I'll speak with him regarding this mix-up.*

Allen scrolled through the names of every person employed at Churchill. There was no Woods; a drill-down search on the last name Woods resulted in a hit—Christopher Woods, corrections officer 1931–1948. Allen opened the file; his entire body went numb. The corrections officer in the black-and-white photograph was the same Woods who escorted Zackary to his office.

Allen walked to his window; for a fleeting moment, he considered jumping through it. Instead, he looked down at the grass-covered courtyard. Don't even think about it. A four-story fall onto soft grass would likely result in severely broken bones and a shit ton of explaining to do.

There was another option, perhaps to bring closure to this insanity.

Allen returned to his desk, locating the Williams address.

Allen had to stop on his way to the Williams house. He didn't feel comfortable driving into the middle of nowhere unarmed, so he quickly stopped at his home to pick up his .45 before setting out.

As Allen turned into his driveway, he noticed Abby's car in the driveway. Parked in his spot was a black convertible Porsche. Now, who the hell is that parked in my spot? Allen thought.

Allen parked at the curb; he glanced at the house before exiting his car. Abby was not on the porch, and neither was the owner of the Porsche. Then, as Allen crossed the lawn, Jacob walked from the side of the house, startling him.

"Jesus Christ, Jacob, what the hell are you doing here?"

Jacob slowly shook his head. "Doctor, I don't think you should go in there. You won't like what you see."

Allen glanced at the front door. "What are you talking about, Jacob?"

"Doctor, Abbey is in your bedroom with Roger. They've been in there most of the morning."

Allen's hands shook as rage consumed him. "They are in my bedroom?"

"Yup, been in there ever since you left."

Allen unlocked the front door before quietly walking toward his bedroom door. It was partially open. He heard a man's voice.

"I'm going to leave soon, Abbey. I wouldn't want Allen catching me here. It would ruin everything if he found out."

Abbey laughed. "He won't catch you here. He stays late at work every day."

"All the same, I better go. I'm sure the neighbors are already suspicious."

Allen stepped into his office, removing the .45 from the top drawer of his desk. I've got nothing more to lose, he thought as he approached the bedroom door. He hesitated before kicking the door open.

Roger turned to look at him. "Hello, Dr. Cre—" Before he could finish his sentence, Allen fired two rounds into his forehead, spattering the now-screaming Abbey beside him. Allen followed by firing a single round into Abbey's chest, sending her sprawling on the floor beside Roger.

As Abbey gasped on the floor, Allen noticed photo albums open on the bed. Abbey reached out to Allen. "Allen, we were planning your birthday."

Allen felt as if a train had struck him. He had forgotten his birthday was this weekend. Abbey wasn't cheating on him. Roger was the event planner. Allen dropped the gun as he realized the severity of his actions. He knelt, rocking Abbey in his arms. "Oh my god, no, Abbey, I'm sorry. Don't die, love. I'll call for help. I'll fix this."

Abbey didn't respond. He turned her bloodied face toward his. She was dead. He had killed his only love in a fit of irrational rage. He had truly lost everything that ever mattered to him.

Allen picked up the gun before staggering to his car. He was going to the Williams house. As he drove from the neighborhood, he had only one thought. He would burn the Williams house to the ground.

As Allen slowly drove up the rutted driveway, he had the unsettling feeling unseen sentries were watching him. He glanced at the rear-view mirror, half expecting to see he was being followed, and he was—by a thick cloud of dust. He thought, Jesus, Allen, get a grip of yourself. The only thing following you will soon be an army of police when they discover what you have done.

Allen stopped when the trees opened, revealing the Williams house in the distance. He expected to find the place boarded up; instead, it looked as it had when crime scene photographs were taken.

Allen continued before stopping in front of the porch. When he reached the top step, something moved above him. He glanced up; a tattered curtain lazily fluttered from a partially open window. From the description Zackary had detailed, he presumed the open window must be the location of Zackary's former bedroom.

Allen hesitated at the front door before turning the doorknob. To his surprise, the door was not locked. Cautiously, he peered inside before entering; all the furnishings remained.

"Why the hell would they have left all the furniture here?" Thought Allen. It looked as if someone still lived there.

A click came from the kitchen area, followed by a low humming. As Allen walked into the kitchen, he realized the sound had come from the refrigerator. He placed his hand on its cool surface before opening the door. A dim light flickered, illuminating its contents: a half-gallon of milk, a carton of eggs, and various condiments. Curiosity drove him to open the milk and smell it. It was fresh. Allen replaced the milk and quickly closed the door. Someone was living here.

Allen glanced out the window above the dripping sink. No one was in the yard, and no car was driving up the driveway. He quickly looked around the place; the last thing he wanted to do was burn the house to the ground with an innocent person or persons inside. He had already killed two innocent people for nothing.

As Allen walked past the gaping opening of the cellar, he felt cool air emitting from the darkness. He paused before deciding not to walk into its murky depths. It was bad enough he was snooping around a possibly occupied house; going into the cellar was not going to happen.

Allen stopped at the foot of the staircase. Other than the voice in his head saying to leave, all was silent. He glanced over his shoulder before carefully moving toward the bedrooms above. Just as Zackary told him, the stairs creaked under his feet as he made his way to the top landing. He glanced down the hallway toward Charlie and Darleen's bedroom. No evidence of a bloody homicide remained.

Zackary's bedroom door was halfway open. Allen felt the breeze coming in through the open bedroom window. He peered around the doorway, expecting to see the bloodstained mattress. Instead, he discovered a neatly made bed. Beside it, sitting on a nightstand, was the Darth Vader lamp.

What the hell? Where's the bloody mattress? Allen stepped closer to the bed before pulling back the blankets. The mattress was clean.

Allen hurried out of the room before entering Darleen and Charlie's bedroom. The bed was clean and neatly made, with a stack of folded laundry on the comforter. Allen could not make sense of what he was seeing. Did someone buy the house? If so, what kind of sick person would want to live in a home where multiple people had been butchered? More out of habit than anything else, Allen began trying to psychoanalyze the type of person or persons who would choose to live here.

The sound of voices outside suddenly interrupted his train of thought. He looked out the bedroom window. In front of his car stood two men with their backs turned to him. They were discussing something. Allen could not make out what was being said. Damn, it has to be the new homeowners. How the hell am I going to explain trespassing in their home?

Allen tried to think of a reasonable excuse. He heard a car door shut. He looked out the window. A man was walking from his driver's door while the other opened the hood. Oh, hell no. Allen left the room, dashing to the front door. He would worry about an excuse later. Right now, he was more concerned with the two men possibly trying to steal his only means of escape.

Allen burst out the front door. "Hey there, gentlemen. That's my car. I seem to have got myself lost—"

The two men turned around. To Allen's horror, one was Zackary, and the other was Jacob.

Jacob smiled as he held up a twisted ball of wires. "Looks like you got some engine troubles, sir."

Zackary nodded. "Yes, sir. Jacob, it looks like ole Dr. Creed will be staying with us for quite some time."

Epilogue

Responding officers at the Creed residence discovered Abby Creed and Roger Moore dead in the master bedroom.

There was no sign of Dr. Creed. However, witnesses in the neighborhood stated they had seen Dr. Creed as he ran from the house and into his vehicle before speeding from the neighborhood.

Two weeks later, a group of teenagers discovered Allen's vehicle parked in front of the Williams house. After a lengthy search of the property, detectives found Allen's remains a quarter mile from the house. A police tracking K-9 located one of Allen's shoes near the location of his body, suggesting he had been running before he collapsed. The medical examiner who performed the autopsy of Allen's body determined the likely cause of death was a heart attack.

Once a respected psychologist and devoted husband, Dr. Allen Creed was laid to rest in a simple grave. Churchill's medical director destroyed a plaque commemorating his tenure at Churchill. The murders he had committed overshadowed his accomplishments. He was no longer known as Dr. Creed. He was Dr. Death.

Dr. Death stared out the kitchen window of the Williams house, his eternal prison. An overweight real estate agent parked his car in front of the house before hurriedly opening his car doors for the new owners of the Williams property.

Made in the USA
Las Vegas, NV
20 December 2024

14972396R00120